Hush, It's a Game

ALSO AVAILABLE BY PATRICIA CARLON

The Souvenir
The Whispering Wall
The Running Woman
Crime of Silence
The Price of an Orphan
The Unquiet Night
Death by Demonstration

Hush, It's a Game

Patricia Carlon

First Published in Great Britain by Hodder and Stoughton

First published in the United States by
Soho Press, Inc.
853 Broadway
New York, NY 10003

Printed in the United States of America

Library of Congress Cataloging-in-Publication Data
Carlon, Patricia, 1927–
Hush, it's a game / Patricia Carlon.
p. cm.
ISBN 1-56947-245-9 (alk. paper)
1. Children—Crimes against—Fiction. 2. Children as witnesses—Fiction. 3. Murderers—Fiction. I. Title.
PR9619.3.C37 H87 2001
823'.914—dc21 00-033910

10 9 8 7 6 5 4 3 2 1

CHAPTER ONE

For the six months of his parole, an observer would have sworn Aldan was intent on one thing only, to start a new life. He had left prison knowing that his long interviews with doctors and clergymen had been faithfully recorded, filed away with the notation that his hatred of Isobel had died away and had been replaced by shame, contrition and indifference to her present whereabouts.

He could still hear in memory his own voice, speaking solemnly into quiet prison air, slowly building up a certainty from supervision for himself once he was released. "It was jealousy you see, sirs. I thought there was another man. Maybe I was wrong. I still don't know for certain, but now it doesn't seem to matter. Funny to think I nearly killed her, put myself here and yet, she doesn't even matter now. I expect that's hurt pride in a way, would you say so, sirs? She told me, that last day, what she thought of me, you see. It was partly how I'd thought actually—she'd hung on to me for what she could get. Till someone better came along, I suppose. I thought so. I don't know for certain. It doesn't matter now. I got suspicious you see, when I was free of my wife Greta, at last, and Isobel ... she hedged, and ... well, you'd have thought she'd have wanted to rush straight to the altar, wouldn't you? But no. She reckoned a few words said over us wouldn't make any difference. It didn't seem ... right to me. Would it to you? Sure, we'd been living together for three years, but that was because I couldn't get free and we didn't want to wait apart. But when I *was* free ... it seemed all wrong to me when she said no to our wedding."

He had thought since that the worst part of the whole business was that he hadn't been suspicious at all. Oh yes, he'd been surprised when the divorce papers had come and Isobel had simply said, "Well, it doesn't make any difference does it? Not really, Frank. We're married already in our own opinions and who else's opinion counts?"

Why hadn't he suspected then that she wanted a way clear and straight in front of her to shed him as soon as she liked? He still didn't know. Perhaps custom—the sameness of having her always there, working together with her, had dulled his sense of danger, letting him think that things would never change.

He'd said simply, "Have it your own way," and she'd smiled, that pursed-lip smile that touched her small thin features with self-satisfaction.

The smile should have put him on guard, too, he had thought afterwards—it should have warned him that she had a special feeling of satisfaction in him agreeing so readily. But he'd simply smiled back and the days had drifted on till the morning he'd woken and found her gone with the money.

He hadn't known that fact at first. She'd left no note or explanation. She had simply been gone, but she had pointedly left open every closet door so his waking eyes should see her clothes and possessions were gone, too.

He hadn't understood even then, not till he'd gone to the store and found she'd left there, too; not till he'd wondered if she was gone for good and if she'd drawn any money from their joint account; not till he'd been to the bank and found the account closed.

He had seen, in the clerk's startled, frightened eyes, what had been in his own face. He hadn't tried to smooth things over, but had simply turned on his heel, and walked out, thinking only of finding her, of getting the money and making her pay for her duplicity.

Finding her had been laughably easy. At first he had thought of her heading straight for interstate where she could disappear so easily. He had sat throughout the night smoking, thinking of her likes and dislikes, where she might head, what she might do. It had come back to memory then

—her almost crazy keenness on opera, her thrill over the then current opera season, her groaning at the price of a season ticket, but her purchase of it all the same.

He had thought then of the streak of meanness in her. He had thought it a good trait enough, that determination to have every pennyworth's value out of everything she bought, and that night he had been sure that if she was still somewhere in the city she'd use the ticket for the final two operas of the season. Her streak of meanness combined with her craze for opera wouldn't let her pass up the chance.

It had been a start towards finding her, anyway. He hadn't been able to think of any other lead, but he'd gone to the theatre without any real hope of finding her, sure that some other city would hold her by then.

Yet she hadn't gone interstate. She'd been there at the theatre, in the middle of the crowd coming out. He'd mingled with it, followed after her, grasped her arm and dragged her to the car before she'd gotten over the first open-mouthed shock.

Jealousy had been his explanation to the police, because truth would have made his sentence the harsher. It wouldn't have gained him back a penny of the money either. He'd screwed out of her, before he'd attacked her, that the cash was salted away. He had known she could deny all knowledge of it and could claim he had forced her to help him and when she'd finally baulked and left him he'd caught up with her and beaten her up because she wouldn't return and go on with the game.

He had left the explanation at jealousy and Isobel had stood up in court, eyes downcast, thin small face quivering, hands twisting at black gloves, saying in her smooth little voice that yes, Frank had always been terribly jealous. There was no truth, of course, in there being another man. She wasn't that sort, but she couldn't get that into Frank's head. He was always imagining things which was why she'd refused to marry him when he was finally free of his wife.

She had had three years of his jealous scenes by then and had been tired of them. Why, he'd even been jealous of the men at work, she'd said quiveringly. So much so she'd had to keep changing jobs to satisfy him.

He had admired her then, even while he'd hated her, because the lie had neatly explained her constant job changing if the police, probing into her background along with his own, had wondered about that.

He had left the dock with her voice crying after him, "I never, never want to see him again!" promising himself that she should and that they'd meet alone.

He had known that even with his protests in prison, she'd be afraid of his release day and would seek out some form of protection—a watch on himself to see what he'd do about tracing her.

Patiently, apparently ignoring her existence, he had gone through the hands of the Prisoners' Aid Society, working steadily at the job they had found for him, and taking the modest room they had also found and he had, as a final touch that had made him sometimes chuckle in the night, solemnly paid out to Greta, his divorced wife, the alimony the court had awarded her.

He had returned to the apparent model of respectability he had been before the night he had sent Isobel to hospital with a fractured skull, and as he knew quite well, Isobel was behaving in a similar fashion.

It had been simple enough to get a prisoner going out, granted freedom, to take a message to contacts outside, to start a search and watch on her. When he came out he had simply phoned a number, been given all available information on her, and had sat back to work and wait till he could get her alone, without interference.

He had long ago, with firm finality, put the idea of the money out of his head. He had known, quite definitely, that by the time he came out, Isobel would have dealt with it in her coolly efficient manner, so that he could never touch it.

He had even been able to approve, quite calmly, her wisdom of the purchase of a north shore home unit, and furniture and her investment of the rest in Government bonds that brought her a steady, if small income. She had also gone back to work, apparently respectably this time.

He had wondered, for a while, after sifting the information, if she had found another partner and was working their old dodge, but she seemed completely solitary, and after all, he had thought grimly, with all she had why should she risk imprisonment now? Isobel had always yearned for security—nothing more. A home, a settled income, smart possessions was her idea of heaven on earth.

That, he had reflected in prison, should have been another warning to him. He should have known that his own plans of drifting round the world, footloose, spending as he went, till the money finally ran out, would never appeal to her; that in the end they would have quarrelled over the spending of the money that had been steadily piling up in the bank under the name of Pascoe.

They had decided on that in case they were ever caught, so the police couldn't trace the money and confiscate it, and he'd made it a joint account in case something happened to one of them and a sole survivor was left. He had agreed to that without hesitation, for Isobel's protection. That remembrance was laughable, afterwards.

The whole idea had been his own in the first place. It had come to him years before he'd even met Isobel, when he'd been working in the big stores himself and had seen how stock simply disappeared. The items taken were quickly noticed by the staff, because it was stores policy never to sell the display stock—the staff went to the storerooms behind for an identical model, so that each day should end with the same display as when the store had opened. The countings and checkings at day's end were rigid routine. It had never failed to amaze him that the same rigid routine simply became a shambles behind the scenes. The stockrooms and stock lists were often in such disorder it was never possible, even at stock-taking, to pinpoint exactly what items had vanished—only the difference between the prices paid for things to the wholesalers, and the amount of money flowing in for items bought, told a sorry tale.

Always of course there were checks on the staff. An assistant could never leave the stores with bags unchecked, or parcels unqueried. There was no loophole there, but there was one big enough to earn him a small fortune he was sure, if he could find the right partner.

He'd found that in Isobel. She had been ruthless enough not to baulk at the breaking up of what had been left of his marriage. He had tried her out tentatively with his idea, left her to think about it and finally they had gone into action together.

All through those three years he had kept on his own modest, respectable job as a clerk. Always Isobel was just as apparently respectable. They lived modestly and the only slur that could have been cast on them was the fact Isobel had no right to the use of his name, or the sharing of his home.

Isobel had had the perfect asset, in the shape of two thoroughly respectable references, covering ten years work in big country stores. Faced with them, with her air of thirtyish respectability, her obvious experience and commonsense, no staff manager had hesitated a second in taking her on, and when she had finally left, always within three months, they had been sorry to see her go.

No one remarked anything odd in the fact that during the peak hour rushes in the various city stores where she worked, between one and two and just before closing time, Isobel was often in earnest talk with a man—a man who never looked the same twice running, and that she always finished in an apparent sale to him.

Electrical goods were her speciality. So she claimed. So her references said, and she knew them thoroughly. She was an asset to her department and no one thought anything of seeing her busily packing up yet another shaver, a mixer, a portable radio or TV set, or similar equipment.

The fact that no docket was made out, no money passed, was never remarked in the crush either. There were always plenty of people in the electrical departments at those hours, either just looking and envying, or buying, or comparing brands and prices for future deals. Aldan was never noticed and with his parcel properly wrapped in store paper he simply walked out unchallenged.

Wherever possible it was the display goods that were slipped into the packages, so the disappearances were put down to ordinary shoplifting. Otherwise goods from the stockroom were taken. Never once had their weekly profit been below sixty dollars. The average was away past it. At times such as the weeks before Christmas and anniversary times, or sale days, their takings had soared almost incredibly.

Professional criminals might have laughed and scoffed at the profits compared to such a strength of days and work in their gathering, compared to one breaking in and a ruthless haul, but he and Isobel had been content with the percentage of value of the items which they'd received in the end.

Isobel had earned, he had acknowledged to himself, a right to half of the money they had piled away. But not a right to it all. The idea and the planning had been his own and more than half the work. His had been the job of always appearing as a different person, yet as a man who had about him no outstanding point, no freakish point, that could bring him into notice. Sometimes he had gone from his job in the lunch-hour or after work, to some public lavatory, and combed his thinning dark hair a different way, or used one of the two wigs—one dark, one fair—he'd bought. Occasionally he relied on the use of suntan lotion—at others he powdered his face lightly to appear paler and older. Because his features were so ordinary he had discovered that a change from his usual rimless spectacles to frames of different sorts made an almost incredible difference to his looks and he had collected seven different pairs of assorted shapes and colourings.

Hats made another big change. So did clothes.

Isobel, he knew, had considered it all easy. She had never seemed to understand how much care it needed—how much planning.

The weeks before Christmas had been their time of

greatest gains. Then, with the crowds, disguise was hardly necessary at all, and shoplifting was so bad they could afford to be reckless in the amount they took.

He remembered, this Christmas Eve, as he packed his case and made ready to go, that it was just after that other Christmas, when the Pascoe account was swelled with their seasonal luck, that Isobel had disappeared, stealing everything he'd worked for, along with his dreams of footloose wandering round the world.

He went to the window of the modest room in the little shabby boarding house and stood looking out. The people in the house opposite had put a tired-looking Christmas tree in their front window, decorating it with a confused jumble that downcurved the branches and practically hid the greenery.

Christmas Eve, he reflected, wondering if Isobel was sparing a thought to that other Christmas, and how he had caught up with her afterwards.

If she was, she must now be certain, after the last six months, that he'd given her best and decided to forget all about her. Certainly there was no one watching over her. He had made sure of that by writing a detective agency, enclosing a fee, stating what he wanted, saying he would ring at certain times for the information he wanted.

He knew now she was on her own, with no protection, no real friends and few acquaintances. She was the sort of woman who would never be missed and asked after if she had been invited to some Christmas festivity and failed to turn up. He hadn't even bothered to consider the possibility she might have arranged a party of her own. Nothing of what he had learned of her new life showed that she had changed at all from the Isobel of the past who had considered party-giving a sheer waste of money and time.

Four days, he reflected, still gazing at the tired tree opposite. Four days before she would be due back, with the reopening of the store where she worked, at her job. Even then enquiries about her wouldn't be started at once. After a long holiday break staff absences were notoriously heavy. It could be as long as a week before even the first enquiry was made; longer still before a real attempt was made to find her.

Even the thought of milk bottles piling up outside her door wasn't a worry. At this time of the year people were invited away at the last moment and left without cancelling deliveries. Milkmen were used to it. When they found a filled bottle hadn't been taken in they simply stopped delivering till they were rung up and told to come again.

Four days at least, he thought complacently. By the time she was found he'd be out of the country, settling into a new life, and perhaps the headache that had been there behind his eyes every time he thought of her and the money, would have gone away for good and left him some measure of peace.

You're going to die, Isobel, he told the hot still evening. There was neither anger nor hatred in the quiet whisper. Simply satisfaction, a feel of completeness and rightness in what he was going to do.

CHAPTER TWO

"Don't touch that!"

She stopped, half way between stove and sink, dirty plate in hand, frowning slightly, wondering suddenly how many times she had said that same phrase already. It wasn't as though the kid was much trouble, she reflected. She was a quiet little thing, and this wasn't much fun for her. A six year old ought to be at a party tonight, or getting ready for Santa to come, not stuck alone in a quiet flat with a middle-aged woman who wasn't even used to kids and who had no real idea of how to entertain them.

She looked down into the long-chinned face whose features—huge dark eyes, long nose, big mouth and solid, prominent cheekbones—seemed too big and too clumsy for its small outlines, and said slowly, "You don't have to be so quiet, Virginia, but don't play with things like that glassware. That's crystal. It's valuable. I'll be downright angry if you break any of it, so leave that cupboard alone, and there won't be any grief to any of us. You can help me wash up in a minute. Right?"

The child, one hand against the workbench top, swayed on one foot back and forth, her long straight veil of fair hair flopping over her shoulders. Isobel, watching, knew a rising sense of irritation. Her own sense of order and neatness yearned to reach out for scissors and cut through the thin veil of hair, neatening the straggling ends. She opened her mouth to speak again, but the child said abruptly, "Yes, Miss Stark."

"Tarks," Isobel jerked. "Tarks, not Stark, Virginia."

A slow painful flush mounted under the child's pale skin. Aware of the acute embarrassment and dismay, Isobel made no attempt to allay it, because her thoughts had flown to Frank.

Funny, she thought, that the child never could remember —like Frank. He used to get mixed up at first, but then she'd changed to calling herself Mrs. Aldan, and there'd been no need for the use of her real name. He'd have remembered it though, and remembered it was Tarks and not Stark, into the bargain. Her small mouth compressed a trifle and abruptly she turned towards the sink, so the child couldn't see her face—a small, slim woman of brisk, nervous movements, her hair still dark and neatly waved back from her unlined forehead. Unconsciously as she put the dish on the sink, her hand went up over her pale blue eyes, touching the slight scar there. There was another, a bigger one, under the dark hair and suddenly, in spite of the closed-in warmth of the small kitchen, she shivered.

She'd always suspected that under his quiet, smooth manner, Frank had had a temper. Certainly she'd known he'd be angry and would try to find her, but she'd thought she was safe. The city had seemed the best place of all to hide till she settled on a place to live and bought a home.

She sighed. She couldn't remember much of that evening when he'd caught up with her. Perhaps that was a mercy. But all the time he'd been in prison she'd been frightened of the day when he eventually came out.

Over and over she'd gone into plans. If she'd been able to think of a way of getting the money out of the country she would have left, but to transfer that amount needed a whole pile of paper work, a whole pile of questions, a whole enquiry as to where and when she'd earned or gained the money ... it had frightened the life out of her. She had pictured herself caught up in government red tape, with police questions to follow, and maybe even the loss of the whole sum in the end.

She had had to settle for staying where she was. She hadn't even tried going interstate, not after she had been given a tip from someone they'd used in the past in disposing of stolen stuff—a tip that Frank had started enquiries about her through another contact. She had faced facts calmly, knowing that to run and keep running was to force herself into a lifetime nightmare when she'd be afraid to go out, afraid to meet a pair of eyes she knew or hear a voice that might later speak her name to Frank. She had finally decided to stick boldly to her own name, settle herself in the city, and simply wait. She had even gone so far as to inform the man who had tipped her off to Frank's enquiries, that she had purchased the flat and furniture and invested in long term bonds, in the hope the news would trickle back to Frank and he would know that the money was untouchable, not simply sitting around in an old sock for his violent removal.

There had been many nights over those long three years of his imprisonment when she'd lain awake, thinking over the day when he would finally turn up on her doorstep. She hadn't expected he would try violence again. She *had* expected a shake-down of some sort—an attempt at blackmail. She had realised how insufferable he could make her life by simply turning up at her place of work, hinting and whispering among fellow assistants and management, but she had decided that to pay anything at all would simply lead down the road to a point where there would be no limit at all to his demands.

As soon as he asks I'll lift the phone and ring the police.

She had told herself that over and over again. Ring the police. Don't hesitate a moment. Simply ring them. And report him.

Frank wouldn't, she knew, tell the real reason for his presence. That would immediately get him into further trouble. She'd simply tell them that he'd tried getting money out of her, that he'd threatened her and she wanted him kept off her doorstep.

He'd be marked after that. The police would keep an eye on him. If he came back, she'd ring them again. Every step towards her he took would simply be against his own interests. He'd realise that in the end and leave her in peace.

She was sure of that. As sure as she was that once he was released it would be a matter of days before he was on her doorstep.

The fact he hadn't come had proved more nervewracking than any attempt at blackmailing, any threat. She had found it incredible, almost . . . indecent, somehow, as though his ignoring her was an insult. In the end she had put a detective agency onto him to find out what he was up to.

The report had puzzled her at first, but as the days had gone on she had simply given into the sweet sense of relief, of freedom. She had told herself happily that he had had the common sense to realise what would happen if he came. He had worked out her reaction along the same lines as she had done, realised there was nothing in it for him but trouble if he pestered her, and had decided to ignore her existence.

She had even speculated, as the weeks had turned into months of freedom, if he was searching for another partner to help him build up yet another nest egg.

The thought returned to her now, together with another.

She said sharply, "Eggs!" and whipped round, frowning as she turned off the heat under the eggs that had been hard-boiling for tomorrow's dinner.

She had decided that not even for the child's sake was she going through the misery of cooking a boiling hot Christmas dinner and then eating it with pretended enjoyment. She'd already done a chicken. Tomorrow she and the child would have that and ham and salad and jellied fruits—would take them to one of the beaches if the weather was right, or if not, stay indoors.

Looking at the child again, at her constant swinging back and forth, one hand on the bench top, she asked in sudden exasperation, "Virginia, what do you *do* on Christmas Eve? Usually?"

Dredged up from her own childhood came the rigid routine of helping stuff the Christmas day turkey, then church going, carol singing, finding the biggest pillow cases in the house, hanging them up, putting out presents round the tree . . .

She asked sharply, when there was no reply, "What do you *do*. Everyone has some sort of routine they chase after Christmas Eve. Every year it's . . ."

The child stopped swinging. She asked, "What do *you* do, Miss Tarks?"

The brief hesitation before the name irritated Isobel. So did the question, because it brought a burning sense of loss, of yearning for those old days when every Christmas Eve was full to the brim, when everyone grumbled about doing the same old things, but protested bitterly if one simple item was altered or forgotten.

Now there was no routine because there was only herself to consider and think about. Every Christmas, since Frank had gone to prison, she had told herself, weeks before, to do this or that, order so many things and do so many more, but when the time came she'd lost interest and Christmas Eve had been like any other evening when the store work was over and free days stretched ahead.

At least though this year she had had a tree. The child was responsible for that. Arthur Segal had brought up the already decorated tree from the flat below first thing that morning.

He had nearly made her late for work, too, with his insisting on going on standing there, wanting to explain all over again just how it was and why he simply had to go north for Christmas and desert his small daughter.

"It could mean big business." The reverence in his voice had both amused and irritated her. "And promotion and maybe a better school for Ginny. Miss Tarks, I just hate imposing on you this fashion, but if you could understand all the implications of this invitation . . ."

He had talked on, firmly rooted to the wine red carpet of her tiny hall, a man of medium height and medium weight; a little man of a medium income he was hoping would be drastically raised in the near future, once he'd accepted this Christmas request to go north with his boss and discuss business right over the holiday.

She had had practically to push him out in the end, reassuring him impatiently that of course she realised there would be no place in the invitation for Virginia, and that she quite understood that lots of people had no relations to help out; that she knew most of the other Court residents would be going away or having friends to stay; assuring him, trying to gild the bitterness of the words, that no, she had no Christmas plans of her own.

Although it was school holidays, the child had been at a day crèche to keep her out of mischief. There'd been no need to worry about her till after work, when Isobel had collected her and brought her back and now ... now the child was repeating her question, Isobel realised, and was gazing at her, eyes bright with curiosity and speculation.

She said helplessly, "I? Oh nothing much. Attend the carol services, have ... well, maybe drop in on friends for a drink—the sort of things your father does, I expect, hmmm?"

The child said reprovingly, "He doesn't go out and leave me alone and he doesn't take me to grown-up parties." She tossed the fine veil of fair hair, and said rapidly, "We go into the city. After dark. And we walk and walk and walk all around the streets, looking in the shop windows at all the pretty things and the storybook people playing in those ... those..."

"Animated tableaux?" Isobel responded automatically. Her thoughts were far away. That had been part of the old routine, she thought, and the desire for the old days was so strong again it was a hard lump in her chest. Wasn't there something, she wondered, something someone had written ... a plea to passing time to turn backwards and make the pleader a child again just for one night? She wondered if the writer had stood as she was doing, listening to a childish voice babbling, remembering the solemn procession up and down brilliantly lit streets. Not city ones, of course, but they'd always gone to the nearest big town and come home with their eyes as round as saucers...

It was a sheer relief when the door bell rang, a relief to let thought and memories be broken, to hurry away from the child's voice and her memories. She didn't bother sliding aside the Judas panel in the door and gazing out first—a habit she'd fallen into after Frank's release. She simply took off the chain and threw the door wide, not really seeing the caller at first, because her mind was concerned and anxious, over the noise that had come from the kitchen as she'd burst back the bolt—a sound that had been suspiciously like cracking glass.

Then her gaze focused and she was backing, while Frank came after her, into the little hall, thrusting the door closed behind him.

CHAPTER THREE

The temptation had been there all along. She had yearned to touch the glass tumblers and bowls again, to hold them in her hands and slowly turn them so that the engravings—flowers and fruit and even little people and country scenes on one or two—could be clearly seen. Virginia had never before seen such glassware—downstairs in the Segal flat it was all ordinary plain and heavy stuff because her father complained the daily women were ham-hands and she herself was too small-fingered to deal carefully with good glass.

Temptation was there and flared up at the ring of the doorbell and the woman hastening away. A caller meant a minute or two at least—time to either get rid of them or welcome them inside and sit them down before talking of drinks or coffee or a slice of cake. She knew that quite well and her hands darted to the cupboard knob and turned it, pulled it. Then she was reaching for the big bowl she had barely just touched before.

Afterwards she told herself it wasn't her fault. It was Miss Tarks' own fault. She said don't touch instead of bringing it out and letting her visitor see it. The cupboard had been shut on it and temptation had grown and grown and grown, quite unbearably.

It had looked so frail a thing she had expected it to be light, like a handful of candy floss and instead it had been heavy—so heavy it simply slid out of her small grasping hands and fell.

Into her ears came the warning voice again, "I'd get downright angry if you broke any of it..." and slow, burning, appalled tears welled up in her eyes. She knew quite well what the words meant—a succession of housekeepers, daily women and Lady Helps had shown her quite plainly.

Of them all she considered Lady Helps were the worst. They were the ones who, as soon as her father's back was turned, were telling her they weren't children's nurses, and she'd better turn to and do her fair share of the housework. Or Else. She knew what that meant, too. A clip of a hard-knuckled hand across her cheek.

If she did something wrong the housekeepers locked her up in her room. She didn't really mind that. Or the daily women who promptly thrust her outside the door till they were finished cleaning, but Lady Helps were different. They didn't believe in locking children up or thrusting them outdoors like puppies who'd wet the carpet. Either punishment meant the loss of a pair of hands that could be put to good use in cleaning and dusting and peeling vegetables. They believed instead in a good clip to each ear, a smart slap on the bottom, and good hard work.

Virginia, in the last couple of years, since she had become aware of the differences in people, had come to divide everyone into one of five groups. Father people were rare. So were Teacher people. They smelt of rose-scented soap, wore rings and if you were lucky and they weren't busy, they tried to show you how to knit or sew. Housekeepers, Daily Women and Lady Helps were commoners and she was quite sure Miss Tarks belonged in the last group.

All the signs were there—the almost terrible neatness of person and surroundings, the long, searching looks of suspicion, the brisk voice giving orders and offering such supposed delights as helping with washing up.

She knew what was going to happen when Miss Tarks came back to the kitchen. A clip to her right ear, another to her left and a hard stinging slap to her rear, then a tight voice saying, "All right, Virginia, if you want punishment, you'll get it, my lady. Down you get and scrub up the floor. And ... no unwrapping your gifts till the holiday season's right over!"

The last threat was an appalling flight of imagination that popped into her head and refused to be put out. She knew it would happen like that. She knew quite positively.

There was always a final stinging punishment and what better and bigger one than that? Miss Tarks had said the glass was valuable. She'd look for something Virginia valued and take it off her. That was a certainty.

The tears rolled quietly down her pale cheeks.

. . .

At first she thought him merely a man, a stranger, and between fright and outrage she opened her mouth to start yelling, and then she was back in the past, remembering, because though the man wasn't Frank as he ought to be, she'd seen him plenty of times when he'd changed his appearance for their racket in the stores. She always knew him by his eyes and hands.

She knew him now even though his hair was dark brown, not greying, and he'd touched up his eyebrows too so that they were reddish-brown. She found herself, strangely enough, admiring that touch because it made such a difference to his face. That and the square framed spectacles.

He said, smiling at her, "Hullo, Is."

She jerked in astonishment, "You've lost your teeth. I. . ." then stopped.

He broadened the smile so she could see the white gleaming set in his upper jaw, that took the place of his own teeth with their mass of gold fillings at the front.

Then he said softly, "They took my own in prison, and handed me a complete set. I've a lower plate too. It's not really comfortable. But it was free. They look after you well inside, Is. Funny, isn't it? They pull out a man's teeth and give him a brand new lot, let the doctors repair and patch him from top to toe, feed him three meals a day and see he goes to bed nice and early . . . even educate him if he likes. You're looked after from A to Z, all without paying a penny. Outside you can have any tooth in your head rot and your insides tie into knots and never know two and two equals four and so long as you pay your taxes on time the government doesn't care a jot.

"Ever think like that?"

She licked at her lips and managed, "No."

He nodded slowly. "I guess you've never had time. In prison now, it's different. You've got lots of time. From sunset to sunrise, all alone in your little cell. You read and you smoke and you sleep a bit, but mostly you think."

She said sharply, "Well if you ever thought about me, Frank, I hope it was with sense to know there's nothing for you here. Why've you come?"

The dyed brows shot up. "Why shouldn't I have come on Christmas Eve to say Merry Christmas?"

She moved impatiently. "Because it would be downright ridiculous, considering how we parted last. If you've come after money, Frank, you can forget it. If you've come, thinking I'll turn all sentimental at this time of the year and be talked into a partnership again and let you get your hands on the money and that, well ... forget that, too. And if you've come to threaten..."

The dyed brows shot up again above the thick dark frames of his spectacles, rounding his grey eyes and lifting the usual droop of his heavy lids.

"I wouldn't *threaten* you, Is," he said softly.

She knew her breath, her whole body, was relaxing. She stood gazing at him silently a moment, then said helplessly, "All right, what is it, then?"

"Can I have a look round the place?"

He didn't wait for permission, but started moving so that she had to go backwards or have his body press up against her own. In the sitting room his gaze flickered round, and he moved across, heading for the kitchen.

She remembered the child then. The last of her fright and rigidity slid away. The child was a guarantee there wouldn't be any trouble. In spite of his smoothness, his protests, she didn't believe he'd come just to stickybeak round the place or wish her seasonal compliments. He wasn't the type. There'd been his first words, too. All about prison that had been, telling her what it was like in there. She didn't fool herself that the expression in his eyes then had been pleasure.

She nearly cried out in surprise when he stood there in the kitchen doorway and merely said, "A nice little set-up," and turned back, with no mention of the child.

Virginia must have crossed the living room, she thought in confusion, while they'd been in the hall. She must have crossed it and entered the bathroom or one of the two small bedrooms. But in a moment Frank was crossing that way and going through the other rooms and coming back, saying again, "A nice little set-up, Is," with still no mention of the child and no sound from her either.

He said then, "Aren't you going to ask me to sit down?"

She hesitated, shrugged, her mind still half on the child's whereabouts. She said almost indifferently, "You can if you like. Wait while I switch off the heat on the stove. I was cooking."

She crossed the deep pile of carpet, thrust open the door and went into the neat kitchen.

. . .

Virginia had known it mustn't happen. The thought of her presents kept hidden till the holiday was completely over was quite unbearable. She knelt, with the tears still welling, mistily groping for the two halves of the bowl, gathering them and then, because the door was opening and she couldn't face the woman or the stinging slaps and the harsh punishment that would follow—because she wanted to put off for the moment the coming of trouble; because she was praying that some miracle would happen and she'd look at the bowl when her eyes cleared and find it was all a mistake after all and the glass wasn't broken at all—she slipped sideways, still holding the bowl, and disappeared from sight under the workbench.

She didn't think of the future, merely of the present moment. It was simply sufficient that for the moment right there and then her ears weren't clipped and her bottom slapped and further punishment doled out. She knelt there, her tears stopped, and her eyes clearing, seeing the corner of the door pushed further inwards and then legs appear—

dark-clad legs. A man's legs. For one moment she had a wonderful idea that her father was back unexpectedly and Christmas was going to be really Christmas after all, with the walk through the city streets among all the wonderful lights and carols, and later hanging up a stocking.

Then she heard a strange voice saying, "A nice little set-up," and the feet turned and moved out the doorway again.

She let her pent breath relax and sat back on her heels to think. A visitor, she realised in a moment, meant reprieve. The Lady Help type never gave you a clip on the ear and a smack on the bottom in public. They were smooth as cream then. So for a while at least she was safe. They didn't have even the chance to ask the automatic suspicious, "Now what've *you* been up to while I was out of here?"

She slid out from under the workbench cautiously, leaving the bowl, kneeling to press it right out of sight at the back. With a visitor there Miss Tarks wasn't going to start sweeping under the furniture. She was going to be all butter-smooth voice and pleasant smiles for a bit.

As Virginia stood upright again, rubbing her hands down the sides of her pinafore, steps sounded and the woman came hurrying in. Her face, to the child's eyes, was oddly flushed, as though she'd been running.

For an instant the two of them stood, simply gazing at one another, then the little hard lump that jumped up and down in Isobel Tarks' thin throat when she talked, began to move. Virginia watched it, fascinated as always, as the woman whispered, "Hush, it's a game. Hide. Till I come. It's ... it's a secret game."

She had closed the door behind her when she came in. Now she opened it again, went out and Virginia heard the man's voice say, "You've fetched out a plate to throw at ..." then the sound was cut off by the closing door again and she was alone, puzzled, silently pondering, bewildered but satisfied that again for the present moment justice wasn't going to be meted out.

. . .

Isobel whispered the words while trying to make sense out of things. She had heard a whisper of sound as she'd pushed the kitchen door inwards, then had seen the child standing still by the workbench, rubbing her hands, guilt all over her face. She had thought in sudden amazement, Good heavens, she must have been under the workbench, while her main thoughts were still concentrated on Frank. She tried to think what mischief the child could have been up to then gave the problem away for the moment. All she could think of then was that she didn't want the child interfering, or listening at a half-open door while she talked to Frank.

She whispered the first thing that came into her head, remembering again her own childhood, when on Christmas Eve someone would come with parcels and someone else in the know would rush ahead, bundling the children out of the way, crying, "Hush, it's a game. Hide! Quick. Till I come. It's a secret game," and there would be a scatter of giggling, excited children.

She went out again, closing the door, twisting the key in the lock behind her so that the child couldn't edge the door half open and listen.

She answered Frank's question with a curt, "I paid good money for my dishes, Frank Aldan. I don't intend smashing them over your head," and realised she'd chosen the wrong thing to say.

"You paid my money for them, Is," he retorted coldly.

"I worked for it. The main risk was mine. I would have fetched a longer imprisonment than you if we'd been caught. You know it. You acknowledged it right at the start when we first tilted at it. They'd have said it was my idea. I was a trusted assistant. You'd have been the outsider. The store would have pressed for the very maximum term for me. You know it." She went on in a sudden fury of words, "You knew it, but you never once listened to me, or asked me, or thought about how I'd like the money spent in the end. It was always yourself you thought about."

"Why didn't you settle for half?" he asked quite mildly.

She didn't answer. There wasn't anything to say. The

truth—that she couldn't have borne to leave the rest of it there in the bank, to be frittered away in his bumming his way round the world, wouldn't have made him feel any better.

She said flatly, "Anyway, it's all tied up now. Tied up solid as wire knots, Frank, and there's no use you thinking you can get at it. Think of what you did to me! You owe me plenty for that. Don't you? I don't owe you anything now. With what you did to me we're even."

"You were always a wonderful talker, Is. That's why you made such a good sales lady. You could talk a customer into believing black was white. The trouble is that while you were talking you'd talk yourself into believing it, too. You owe me plenty, Is. Three years and ten months of my life. Where's my compensation for that?"

"That's crazy," she gave back. "You fetched that through your own fool-headedness. I didn't ask you to hit me." Remembrance of that last meeting was clear now, and frightening. She abruptly jerked to her feet, saying, "We've nothing to say any more. You'd better go." When he didn't move she asked in rising irritation and panic, "Why'd you come?"

"To say goodbye."

As her mouth rounded in surprise he nodded. "You see, Is, I've been on parole these last six months. That means reporting to the police, doing what they'd approve of. I had remission for good conduct and so on. That meant I didn't serve what the judge handed out. But it meant parole when they did let me out. But that's over now. I can go where I like and start a new life." He touched his hair. "I'm quite grey now. Iron grey. This is to make me look younger. And I'm taking a new name too. And leaving the country. Tonight. Starting off fresh as you might say." He smiled, showing the brightly white new false teeth. "Life begins at forty five, eh, Is?"

It was the last thing she had expected, but relief thawed her into a faint warmth towards him, because there wasn't going to be any trouble.

He said, "But first I wanted to say goodbye, Is."

She felt strangely shy, gauche and awkward, caught off balance, not knowing what to say.

Then she saw the gun.

She stood there, staring at it in mild surprise, then lifted her gaze to his face. He didn't look angry, but she half turned. Starting to move, she looked back at him, still bewildered, still surprised. He didn't look as though he hated her. He simply sat there, quite placid of face.

And shot her dead.

CHAPTER FOUR

He stood for a moment looking down at her, and knew only regret. Not for Isobel Tarks. He didn't even think of her as Isobel any more. She was simply a huddled heap of clothes on the floor. His regret was for something gone out of his life. For the past four years he had lived day and night with the thought of reaching her and making her pay. He had filled lonely hours with plans and thoughts of that final meeting, of all he had to do, of the hours he had to wait. Now it was over. He'd never again be able to fill in time with plans. He'd lost something that had become a need, a solace, through the years, and he was simply regretting it.

He sighed, looked at the gun, and then simply dropped it at her side. There was no way of tracing it back to him. No fingerprints on it either because he had handled it through a carefully folded handkerchief.

At the hall doorway he looked back, a long slow look round the room, before he switched off the light and went out through the hall, closing the door behind him.

He was thinking of New Zealand as he made for the lift. He had chosen it because the plane fare was small, yet it was a different country while still being open to him without need of passport or visas. To go somewhere where those were needed he would have been forced to give his name and his record would have been on file for everyone to note. No other country, he had known, would have wanted him with his record. The alternative had been to purchase a forged passport and he had had no spare cash for that. His sole asset, when he had come out, had been the money for his old car. He had asked the solicitor who had acted for him in court to see it was sold and the money banked for him, out of reach of either Greta, his divorced wife, or Isobel. He had come out to find a little over five hundred dollars as a result. That, now in his case in traveller's cheques, was to be the means of starting him off afresh, leaving the police, if they wanted him, to search for him in his own country at first.

He didn't look back as he strode out into the evening. There was still faint light in the sky, though all the buildings were bright with lights. He didn't bother to stop, to gaze up at the tower building of flats and pick out the darkened windows that were Isobel's. He simply walked away, his stride growing faster and faster, his mind on New Zealand, on freedom, or a new land and a new life.

. . . .

She wasn't wrong about Miss Tarks. Virginia was quite sure of that. Miss Tarks wasn't the sort who played games. She was just pretending. There wasn't going to be a wonderful surprise when the door opened. That was nonsense. The woman simply wanted her out of the way and quiet, and not stickybeaking for a while. That was all.

Virginia wrinkled her nose in disgust, then sighed. For the present she was safe, but soon the door was going to open again and what ... what if the visitor was going to have something to eat? Something that needed to be set out beautifully in the glass bowl?

She felt quite sick at the idea. Scrabbling under the workbench, she pulled out the glass, staring at it, then fumblingly she opened the cupboard where spare papers were kept, brought out a whole pile and as carefully as possible she wrapped up the glass.

She was panting when she'd finished, from a combination of tiredness and panic. She wondered what Miss Tarks would say when she found the bowl had disappeared. Perhaps, she thought, and a snuffling giggle caught at the back of her nose, Perhaps she'll accuse me of eating it!

But one thing was certain. She couldn't punish when she didn't know what had happened to the thing—whether perhaps it had been missing for days and days. Why her Daily Woman, if she had one, might even have taken it. Virginia brightened at the thought, while carefully picking up the bundle and going to the far wall.

There was a steel plate there, identical to the one in the Segal flat below, identical to others in every kitchen in the vast tower buildings. You pressed down the catches and the plate flipped down into a little shelf, and you could peer into darkness and feel a cold breath of air come whistling up to touch your bare skin. Virginia had tried it a lot of times. She was fascinated by the one in the Segal flat, and loved watching the parcels of rubbish vanish into gloom.

It was frightening when she found her present parcel was too big to enter the slot. She had to sit down again on the floor and undo it, her hands trembling, terrified the kitchen door would open. In the end, because she heard a sharp loud bang from the other room, she didn't dare wait to wrap up the pieces again. She dropped them, separately, as they were, down the chute, closed it and slipped back the catches.

She stood with her back to it, waiting, but nothing happened. After a while she moved to the door, and slowly pulled at the handle, but she couldn't open the door. She realised after a while that she was locked in. It didn't worry her. It proved what she'd suspected, she thought complacently. Miss Tarks hadn't been playing games. She'd wanted to talk alone with her visitor.

Piqued, Virginia applied one eye to the keyhole, but she couldn't see anything. Not even light.

Puzzled, she stepped back, wondering in astonishment if Miss Tarks had forgotten all about her and had gone out with her visitor to dinner, switching off the light before she left. She decided after a while that it wasn't reasonable.

Miss Tarks had simply gone downstairs, to the foyer of the building. That was it, she thought sagely, pleased with herself for working it out. She'd gone down to see him off, and she'd be up in a few minutes. In the meantime there was no harm in making sure of being in her good graces.

With a sigh Virginia made for the sink, pulling a chair with her so she could kneel on it and manage properly. Hot water swished into the stainless steel bowl and she delighted herself with making as much froth as possible before plunging in her small hands.

After a little while she began singing, Miss Tarks and the crystal bowl both forgotten.

. . .

He should, he thought in rising annoyance, have remembered that on Christmas Eve there'd be families visiting, heading out of town for the holiday season, and that lorries would still be thundering along making last minute deliveries to keep faith with customers who'd ordered for the big day. The roads were choked and five times already the taxi had simply pulled up, the meter ticking away, the squawk box bleating out endlessly with calls and demands and requests from the taxi headquarters, while the driver sat back smoking, ignoring both the bleats and his passenger.

Frank said mildly at last, "Must you have that thing wailing and moaning?"

The driver flicked a glance back, "It's company." His tone implied his silent passenger wasn't.

Still mildly, but feeling his body tightening with held-in temper Frank said, "It's my right to ask for it off if I wish it. Isn't that so, now?"

Burly shoulders shrugged, "Sure mate, it's your right to ask," was the placid retort.

Useless, Frank thought, and held down the temper and irritation and was silent. He was going to get nothing by insisting, except a possible retort that he could always get out and get another taxi. Customers weren't always right any more and the man knew it. Frank wondered in faint amusement what three years and ten months in prison would do to the I'm-the-top-dog-you're-the-mug attitude of the driver, then forgot it in anxiety as the taxi jerked another block, then pulled up again. Nervously he glanced at his watch, tapping worried fingers on his knee.

He jumped when the driver spoke again, then was amused because it was so apparent the other man had abruptly remembered the season and was putting on false friendliness to go with it. "Not to worry mate," he said blithely, "We'll hit Mascot on time. You're for Zealand, aren't you? Going just for a week or two?"

He hesitated, then felt foolish and murmured, "I may stay a while longer. I haven't really decided."

"Well!" The other man exhaled a gusty breath. "You're on a nice wicket. Wish I could dice up my life like that. As it is I'll be working Christmas, right through."

Idly he gave back, "It pays, doesn't it? You'd get big tips this time of the year ..."

"You kiddin'?" The man turned right round to stare at him, then swung back to the wheel and jerked the taxi into motion again, throwing over his shoulder, "We're lucky if we see five cents over the meter. Everyone's skinned out on buying the party grog and presents and turkey."

And that's a hint to me to tip well, Frank thought wearily, and knew he wasn't going to. He grudged the taxi fare, inflated by the traffic jams. He paid it without any tip at all, ignored the man's glare and waved aside the porter, carrying his own case inside, towards the weighing machine and desk.

He never reached either.

A hand touched his arm and he swung round, to look into Greta's round, flushed face.

He stared at her, letting the case slide out of his hand to hit the ground, jarring against his ankle. He went on staring at her, and at the three men who flanked her—his one time father-in-law, his one time brothers-in-law.

Movement came suddenly back. She couldn't know him, he thought confusedly. It was impossible. He looked totally different to Frank Aldan. Why was she touching *his* arm, pulling *him* up?

She said, "I know it's you, Frank. You're the last passenger to check in for that plane, and I can see your name now on that case label."

He stared down stupidly and thought in amazement that the label didn't say Frank Aldan. He hadn't put that by mistake. He'd written Baring, his new name. Great heavens, the woman was mad, he reflected.

He took a step backwards, and the four of them crowded after him, so that they formed a tight, hard little knot right in the middle of the hall. People passed round them, frowning, staring at them.

He got out at last, "My name? My name is Baring. What do you mean?"

"Don't be a fool, Frank." There was all her old asperity in her voice. She hadn't changed a bit, he thought dumbly. She was as big, as fat, as florid and as badly dressed as ever. And as sharp tongued. She'd always treated him as though he were half witted and needed her sharp promptings to help him do anything.

He said stubbornly, bending to grip the suitcase handle again, "My name is Baring. Not Frank. Herbert Baring."

She gave a sudden shriek of laughter. That hadn't changed either, he thought, wincing. It was an atrocious noise. That was what had drawn him to Isobel first—her quiet, soft laugh.

Isobel.

He remembered her for the first time since he'd left Nurrung Court and the silent flat. He was instantly panic-stricken, appalled, because now his safety was threatened—now Greta and her family knew his new name, his new appearance, where he was going.

His lips parted, but she was saying, "Of all the names to choose, Herbert's the limit! Now stop being a fool, Frank. We'd best move into a corner somewhere. We're holding up traffic. Get your case and shift over..."

He said with sudden overwhelming rage and panic, "Get out of my road!"

Her big mouth tightened and downcurved. She said tightly, "Either you do as you're told, Frank, or there's going to be a full blown scene. Stop being a fool. We've got to talk."

There wasn't time to insist he wasn't Frank Aldan. He said, "I can't talk to you. I've got a plane to catch," and he looked up in renewed panic as a voice came from the loudspeaker, calling the passengers for New Zealand. "I have to go. You can see that."

"You're not going anywhere, Frank. Get that into your head." Her hand went out flat against his chest, pushing at him, thrusting him to the corner she had pointed out. "You're not walking out on me, Frank. Dad and me and Foley and Lloyd are here to see to it."

He tried to get round her and the burly figure of big Foley Timmins, but the man blocked him, thrusting him backwards again. He could feel tears of rage, of mortification and sheer agony, pricking at the back of his eyes.

Greta said, "If you fancy a scene, Frank, I'll make one. I'll call a policeman and give you in charge ... for assaulting *me*."

. . .

The basement was a big area, perpetually warm from the incinerator that was lit at least once a day. At Christmas time it seemed never to go out, Robbins thought disgustedly.

He stood beside it, picking moodily with one fingernail at a crevice between his front teeth, telling himself he was sick of the job, sick of Nurrung Court—Court, mind you, he thought in disgust. Sure, it was in the form of a courtyard, but *Court*—nothing courtly about it. It was a big ugly horseshoe shaped tower, and the occupants were big ugly Biddies and Bastards, both words with a capital B and they could think themselves lucky he didn't call them something worse. Moodily, dragging deeply into the crevice and wincing as his nail touched bare gum, he reflected on what he'd made out of Christmas. One dollar. One measly dollar. He could hardly believe it. There were sixty three flats in the Court and he'd received exactly one tip and that for one dollar.

To make matters even worse it wasn't one of the owners who'd tipped him, but just a chap who'd been loaned the home unit while the owner was overseas. Overseas, mind you, he reflected and looked at his nail, shocked to find it bloodied. Pyrrhoea, he thought glumly. That'd mean dollars galore for a dentist, but what did the owners in Nurrung

Court care? All his teeth could flop out and his gums wither to the bone and they wouldn't give a damn.

He'd been downright shocked to discover most of them hadn't so much as known he'd existed. He'd gone round knocking on doors, giving out Merry Christmasses and grinning away, expecting a tip, and nearly all of them had simply stared blankly and asked who the devil he was. When told he was the caretaker who burned their rubbish and swept the court and watered the lawn and saw the cleaning women did their jobs on stairs and landings they'd just said back, "Well I never knew, but Merry Christmas to you, too," and closed their doors.

Nice. Real nice. He poked at another tooth, and wondered what they'd say if the pile of rubbish now in front of him was never burned. Had they imagined, he wondered, that a little black gremlin lived in the basement, to sort out their rubbish and get rid of it? They must have, the surprised way they'd looked at him. And none of them seemed to have remembered that with all their shopping at this time of the year the wrappings and rubbish were coming down to the basement non-stop.

I ought to go on strike, he thought moodily. When they found funny smells coming up their rubbish chutes and went to investigate and found a mountain of decaying rubbish and no one to dispose of it, then they might stop to think he should be getting decent tips for the job. Not just at Christmas either, come to that.

He couldn't get over the way they hadn't known him. Only a few had known him vaguely. Only one...

His mouth tightened. Blast the old biddy. No, not biddy, he reflected. Bitch. She was that, and more. He'd thought he was doing her a favour and instead she'd threatened him with the sack, the police, and everything else he could think of.

Miss Tarks! Miss Blasted Tarks! What if she was quite right about him just using the gas as an excuse to start snooping round her place? He hadn't done any damage or pinched anything either.

He'd told her he was doing his duty. So he had, come to that. There'd been a smell of gas all right and he'd called the Gas Company and they'd come out and gone sniffing around. What if *he* had been the one to suggest it might be Miss Bitchy Tarks had left a gas tap open?

He had his rights and one was a master key to get into the units in case of fire or emergency. He'd used it. Of course there hadn't been anything wrong in there. There'd been a little leak somewhere else. But, as he'd said to her, when she'd come up and found him—he was only doing his duty.

But no—she'd gone half mad. Sworn at him. Told him he could have smelt gas escaping under the front door if there'd been any trouble in her place. She'd threatened with everything she could and that was plenty.

Still, he regarded his bloodied nail sadly, there was no use thinking about it, and maybe there was something worthwhile in the pile in front of him. He brightened at that. Surprising, shocking even, what folks threw out, he reflected. Cups that only needed a handle glued back, bits of pottery, books on which he could get twenty five cents a time.

He bent to the task almost willingly, but stopped almost at once. Well, would anyone believe it, he asked himself. He held the half bowl up to the light. Funny it hadn't smashed to smithereens coming down, but it had landed on a pile of shavings someone else had thrown down. He would have sworn it was Miss Tarks' property, too. He began to pick over the rest of the shavings and came up with the other half, holding them in his big-fingered hands. Miss Tarks' property he was sure. He'd seen the crystal when he'd been in the flat and thought she must have spent a pretty penny on it.

He thought in grim amusement that she must have nearly split her stepins in rage when she'd broken it. How'd she done it, anyway, her with her prissy careful ways? And why toss it out without trying to see if it couldn't be mended—a lot of the big stores could do wonders with anything.

He remembered then and gave a cackle of laughter. The kid! He'd bet anything that damn kid had broken it.

And shot down the pieces so the old girl wouldn't find it.

"Oh you'll catch it!" he said aloud. "She'll find out, and you'll catch it, miss! You won't have appetite for your Christmas dinner when she finds out!"

Carefully he put the pieces aside. She'd probably come down, as soon as she discovered the loss and screwed out of the kid what had happened, but if she wanted the pieces she could pay for them. He'd tell her bluntly they must be in the rubbish and it wasn't his job to sort through it for lost items. She'd have to pay for his time in doing it. He grinned, chuckling, coughing in rasping amusement at the way he'd skin her, and how she'd have to eat humble pie and speak to him cooingly.

Like a dove, he thought and the idea was so funny in connection with Isobel Tarks that he had to sit down to enjoy it.

. . .

Her statement was so outrageous he could feel his neck puffing up, his face turning brick red. His lips parted, but the torrent of rage never had a chance to spill out because Greta was saying crisply, "I mean it, Frank. Dad and Foley and Lloyd will back me up and by the time we've talked to the police and they've taken statements or whatever they do, you won't be able to leave the country no matter how you try. Not till the case comes up. And ... I'll make the case stick, Frank. They'll believe me, after what you did to that woman. Won't they?"

His rage went, leaving only puzzlement.

It showed in his amazed, "What's the matter with you? I haven't harmed you, Greta. You wanted a divorce. You got it. And I've been paying your alimony ever since I was free of prison again."

She nodded, the ribbon trimming on her impossible straw hat jaggling and wobbling in front of his eyes.

"That's just it, Frank. My alimony. That's what we've come about?"

"But I paid it!" It was almost a wail of anguish.

"But what about next week, Frank? And the week after? How am I going to collect with you in another country, disguised, even," her bright blue eyes flickered over him in contempt, "and using another name?

"Oh no, Frank, it won't do. You've even got a one-way ticket. That means you're not coming back."

He'd had so many shocks that that one hardly made any impression on him. So much was incredible, yet had to be swallowed, that he was quite capable now of swallowing the fact she had somehow found out all his plans, even down to his one-way ticket.

The voice called, "Will passengers for New Zealand, Flight 073, please go down to gate No. 4. Will passengers for..."

"Greta!"

"No. We've got to thrash this out, Frank. You can turn your ticket in and get another plane tomorrow or the next day if we sort this out now. I asked at the desk and they were very nice and quite considerate. I said there was grave family news I had to give you and you might have to cancel and they were wonderful. Weren't they dad? Foley? Lloyd?"

Her big greying head turned to each of the men, receiving their affirmative nods.

"Stop having kittens, Frank," she went on briskly. "And now you listen to me. You were bitter as vinegar there in court and you near as made no difference, insulted the judge when he awarded me alimony. You got the rough side of his tongue and you went out of court white faced and nearly biting your lower lip through. But you had to pay. And I'm not going to waste time in talking about the way you shamed me going off with that woman and then beating her up. Let's leave it. But we can't leave the fact that when you were in prison I got nothing. The legal man I went to said that was my hard luck, and never mind. All very nice for him in his cushy office, but I had to live someway. I managed. I knew when you were due out and I was all ready for a big fight to get my rights out of you and bless me, next thing I knew the weekly sum came without a word.

"Well, prison might have changed you," her tone expressed complete disbelief about that, "but I couldn't believe it. Next thing I found out you were on six months parole when you had to keep your nose clean. I said to dad, 'There's the reason. He's not risking having a summons taken out on him at the moment. He's playing at being a good boy, but once that parole's up he's going to skip.'

"Oh yes, Frank, I didn't live with you for twelve years without seeing through you. You were going to light out and leave me flat. This paying up was just to let you have a bit of freedom while you were still on parole—you didn't want anything more in the trouble line.

"So I got in touch with a woman in that boarding house. If it's one thing a woman can't stand, Frank—a decent, respectable woman I mean—it's the type of louse that throws up another decent woman and makes off with someone else.

"I told her the full facts and that I was scared you'd skip. My health's bad and I need my ten dollars and I know how difficult it is to get hold of a husband who skips, and make him pay. I asked her to let me know if you gave notice at the boarding house."

"But I didn't!" He could feel sweat on his face, on his hands, trickling down his legs and back. "I didn't give notice at all."

"No, you just said you'd be away over Christmas. She told me, and I thought, This is it. I asked her to see what she could find out and this morning when you were having your bath, Frank, she went through your pockets." Her voice rose in triumph, "And she found that ticket and where it was for, and the name on it. And she rang me. Now what do you think of that!"

CHAPTER FIVE

The washing up finished, the dishes carefully dried and stacked, Virginia cleaned out the sink, rinsed out the dish-cloth and then sat back to smile in approval, before sliding again from the chair and going over to the door. It was still locked and another look through the keyhole still only showed blackness.

She wondered if she dared eat a few biscuits to pass the time. Solemnly she debated the idea and discarded it. She might make crumbs, and the woman might come back in a hurry and catch her and there'd be a scene. Biscuits before bed was something forbidden she knew, and already it was after seven thirty bedtime.

That was another puzzling fact. The woman had been firm about seven thirty. "Don't think you can stay up a minute later than usual this evening, Virginia. You'd only be over-tired tomorrow and that wouldn't do, would it?" she had said briskly.

And now ... Virginia wondered in sudden excitement if perhaps after all it was a game; that a wonderful, wonderful surprise was coming; a surprise so lovely that bedtime could become elastic for it. Perhaps, she thought hopefully, the stranger had been a friend of her father's, coming to say a wonderful surprise had to be collected. And Miss Tarks had gone to get it. She was being longer than she'd expected to be, that was all.

She began to laugh and because life was suddenly such a happy thing, an exciting thing, she began to sing again, going to the window, sliding back a little and peering out, down into the world of the courtyard far below where Christmas lights were lit on a tree in the court, and gazing at lighted windows across the way and lights dancing on the harbour.

"It's Christmas," she said aloud, "Christmas and I'm having a surprise," and she laughed again from sheer happiness.

. . .

Down already, he thought in satisfaction and decided to have A Back. That was a good thing to have when there was bending to do. It slowed you up considerably and you could jack up the price for the pain. Yes, he'd have A Back. A real, rip-snorter of A Back.

He eased himself in his chair, hand to the base of his spine, rubbing, his face mournful, then swung round in dismay when a voice asked, "How far apart are the pains?"

"Eh?" He stared in astonishment at the stocky figure leaning against the basement door jamb. The big nose, casting a shadow over the face, looked quite enormous, and reflected light made round yellow pools of the glass inside the dark spectacle frames.

Robbins smiled. "You want something, Mr. Warner?" he asked almost affably, remembering his one Christmas tip. Then he frowned, "And what was that you said?"

The young man moved, coming into the basement, becoming, instead of a gargoyle figure, an ordinary thirtyish man with a rather large nose and chin and tired blue eyes behind ordinary spectacles. "I asked how far apart were the pains? You looked as though you were going to give birth."

Robbins gave a snort of amusement, said in slight reproof, "I've got A Back. From all this shifting and burning." He looked with interest at the tiny Christmas tree, bedded in a pot so small it looked more like a teacup than anything. "You won't get that to sit up straight. Not in that pot."

"So I realised. I came down to ask if you had something else I could put it into."

"Well I guess so, if I look." Robbins rose quite briskly, began rooting among the cartons and boxes he kept stacked into one corner, and asked, "You doing some entertaining, Mr. Warner?" because there was possibility of help being needed, if so, and an extra tip in the idea, but he was disappointed.

"No. I'm damned if I know why I bought the thing, except ... it was the last in the shop. It was quite alone." He flashed a sudden grin at the older man. "It didn't seem right—being alone on Christmas eve."

"No," Robbins turned slowly, "It's not right, is it? Being alone tonight."

For a moment they simply stood there, knowing that each was alone. I should ask him up for a drink perhaps, Leigh Warner thought anxiously, but knew he wasn't going to. Robbins was the type to turn maudlin with two drinks and nasty with three, and he'd take the invitation to mean he could become familiar in the future and make a nuisance of himself.

He said suddenly, "I suppose there are quite a lot of people in the Court who are alone tonight, come to that. Are there? Spinsters, widows and so on?"

Robbins blinked, came out of abstraction, shook his head. "Most of them're retired couples. There're just a few like Miss Tarks ... and *she's* not alone tonight either. Got the kid. The Segal kid. The father's away and the mother's dead. Know them?" As the younger man shook his head, Robbins sighed. "She's going to regret it," he nodded to the broken crystal. "The little wretch must've done that and shot it down the chute. Valuable stuff, that is."

Leigh Warner slid the potted tree into the wooden box the older man handed over. He said almost curtly, "Perhaps she finds companionship tonight more valuable still."

"Not her. Not Miss Tarks. She'd put things above people any day've the week. When she finds out all hell's going to break loose. I wouldn't be that kid, not when that happens."

Leigh shrugged. The subject didn't interest him. He said, still with that same curtness, "Thanks. And ... merry Christmas, of course."

"Oh, of course!" Robbins agreed dryly. "And very merries to you, too."

For a moment they gazed at one another silently again, motionless, both pairs of eyes mocking themselves, the other man, the words. Goddamnit, Leigh thought wearily, he knows how false all this is. This tree, and the expressions of goodwill that mean nothing. Tonight and tomorrow I'll sit up there on the fourth floor alone and he'll sit down here, alone, too. What a farce it all is.

He turned sharply, went up the steps, crossed the carpeted, perfect foyer and went into the lift with its artificial tree shining bravely at the back.

On the fourth floor he crossed more carpet, juggled the key into the lock of the flat, went inside, switching on lights as he went over to the sitting room window to flick up the blinds and set the tree on the sill.

He didn't have anything to decorate it with. Untrimmed, it looked faintly pathetic. Cinderella with no ballgown, he thought tiredly. He wished now he had never taken up the offer of the Brentwood's home unit while they were away, during the time he was to be in the city, consulting on the new bridge job. At the time it had seemed heaven-sent, a haven of privacy, but after two months of it he still knew nothing about his neighbours, hardly ever saw them, didn't so much as know their names. The place could have been a prison where every soul went off to its own little cell to dwell untouched by others of its kind. It gave him the shivers, especially tonight. It wasn't even as though he'd chanced to make friends on the job. As consultant, called in because of inefficiency at the top of the job, the men of his own rank resented and avoided him, the rest regarding him as something alien as well as top brass, and leaving him alone, too.

He touched the tree gently. It would have to be his sole Christmas companion. Quickly he slid the window open so that a gentle breeze touched the small living thing. He stood gazing out, at the spurious cheer of the decorated tree down below, at the shining lighted windows all round the court. Behind them were the retired couples Robbins had mentioned, and their friends and perhaps families—children and grandchildren. Even people like this Miss Tarks had someone...

He looked up, half turning. At one window, two floors higher, a little to his left, a figure stood at another window, gazing out, outlined against the lighted room beyond. A child, he realised. Dreaming probably.

He lifted his hand in a half salute. At the other window a small pale hand fluttered, in salutation and greeting. The two hands, one large, one so small, went on waving across the night, across the court.

He started to laugh. How inane it must look to anyone watching, he thought. He wished now he had decorations—he could have sat there and decorated the tree for her pleasure, while she watched. She could have seen fairly clearly what he was doing, he was sure, and it might have amused her.

On impulse he turned, went out of the place again. He'd go back to the stores—there were plenty open late tonight, get some sort of decorations, and trim it. Tomorrow, if she looked out, the tree would be there. She might enjoy it.

And it was something to do. Something to kill the deadly loneliness of a night when it simply wasn't right, or bearable, to be alone.

. . .

"I think you're crazy."

Frank answered her triumphant question with the flat, disgusted statement. He said rapidly, "To do all that, as though ... good god, I'm only going to New Zealand, to ..."

"With a one-way ticket!"

"I'm trying to start a new life. You've said yourself my parole's over. For God's sake, Greta, have something you could call sense ..."

"Mr. Baring!" The loudspeaker broke into sound almost shockingly, "Mr. Baring, passenger for New Zealand. Mr. Baring, Bar ... ing. Would Mr. Baring, passenger for New Zealand, report to gate four? Flight No. 073 is about to depart. Mr. Baring, please report."

"Greta ..."

She went on talking, not heeding either the woman's urging or his frantic attempt to get past them again. The four of them were solid, unmoving, cornering him like a panic-stricken sheep, and Greta was saying, "You were skipping out, Frank, and you're not going to. I know my rights, and I want them. Stop acting like a big baby! I tell you you can change your ticket for another flight as soon as this is worked out. I only want a settlement so I have something to fall back on."

"Settlement?" he whispered, hardly knowing what he was saying.

"A thousand dollars."

He started to laugh. It was suddenly incredibly funny she could stand there, a big, ugly woman, demanding a thousand dollars that he didn't have.

He asked harshly, "Where would I get it?"

"I don't know, but I want it. That's two years payments, Frank. Give it to me and you can go to Hades for all I care. This weekly business is nerve wracking anyway because I've never been able to count on you really paying and not just stopping to spite me till I take out an order against you."

"I don't have any money," he said wearily.

"Mr. Baring, passenger for New Zealand. Are you in the airport, Mr. Baring? Your plane for New Zealand is about to leave."

"Greta...

"I don't have any money, Greta." He tried again to move past her, as though that finished it.

She shook her head. "Then you're not going to New Zealand. I'm pretty sure I can get some sort of court order to stop you leaving till I get some guarantee about alimony. We'd have to ask a lawyer. I can't do that till after Christmas. You needn't look as though you've been hit with a brick. You can make a new life right here, Frank, in a steady job, and send me my money weekly. Or give me a settlement..."

He was so confused, so angry, so frightened, he didn't really know what he was saying. Only a low animal-like wail escaped his lips as the loudspeaker said with cold finality, "Flight 073 is on the tarmac. If you are in the airport, Mr. Baring, please report to the desk as your plane has now left," then he broke into speech, crying desperately, "All I have is a little over five hundred dollars. In traveller's cheques."

He saw the glitter in her eyes and knew what a fool he'd been, then she was saying, "That would cover a year."

He simply stood there, trying to work out what he was going to do, then her father said slowly, "You could take the cheques, Greta. You can't get blood out of a stone. You'd be a year to the good and that'd be something."

"Yes," she agreed, nodding vehemently.

It was the only way, he thought despairingly. Give them the cheques. Get rid of them. Change the ticket for another flight. Get away just the same, though his new identity was no good now. As soon as Isobel's death was in the papers Greta would tell the police and they'd hunt for him in New Zealand, for questioning.

I could change my name again and my looks, he thought confusedly. Wherever I am they'll hunt me, won't they? And, he reflected, his plans still stood in one particular—they couldn't *prove* absolutely that he was the one who'd killed Isobel. Deliberately he hadn't taken a thing from the flat for fear it might be found on him, traced back to him if he sold it. He'd worked out his parole, and wasn't it a natural thing for a man released from that, to give himself a Christmas present of a new name, a new life, a new country?

Even Greta ... didn't it add up he might try to get free of a bloodsucker like Greta, by simply vanishing?

They couldn't prove he'd killed Isobel. That was the point. The main thing was to get rid of Greta and her impossible family so he could think clearly.

Lloyd was saying, "Those things have to be signed in front of the person who cashes them. Isn't that so, Frank?"

"Eh?" His head jerked round, seeing the red beefy face looking at him thoughtfully. "Yes, that's right."

"Then that's a difficulty. You couldn't get a hotel to change that many. Not five hundred dollars worth. We'll have to wait till the banks open in four days, and you can go with Greta then, sign them and she can get the money. Then you can go."

It wasn't possible. She might be found by then, he reflected. He couldn't just sit around waiting to be picked up by the police. He had to have a chance to get free of any questioning at all. He had to.

They were closing round him again. Greta was saying, "You'd best come home with us then." To his ears her sudden agreeableness had a horrible spurious ring of false seasonal cheer. "After all it's Christmas, isn't it, Frank and maybe I've spoilt your big day. You could spend it with us and the holiday and afterwards we could part friends. After all I'm only trying to hold onto what is legally mine. You must admit that."

The thought of being closeted with them for four days nearly made him shriek. The thought of confinement, the inability to get free, was unbearable. He had to be gone before four days were up. He *had* to be. The main thing was to get rid of Greta and her family. He could accept the loss of the money if he only could do the latter.

His thoughts broke out of their chaotic panic. Suddenly he was cool again, content that he could see clearly ahead for a few hours at least.

He said quietly, "You're being ridiculous, Greta. I intended that money to start myself off again in New Zealand. I fully intended to keep up your payments. After all," his face twisted, "I don't fancy having warrants after me and police looking for me. I've had enough of them. But if you're going to stick out for this you can have it. You can hold them for the moment.

"But I'm not coming with you. That'd be a farce. I'll go to a hotel tonight. Tomorrow or Boxing Day, as soon as I can, I'll contact a man I know who'll change the cheques. I'll bring him to your place and sign them then."

CHAPTER SIX

Her lips felt stiff, the skin on her cheeks felt paper thin. If anyone else asked her that blithe question, "And what do *you* want for Christmas?" she was afraid her control was going to break, and she was going to give back, "Freedom. A chance never to smile a false smile; never to speak again those meaningless words, 'Oh yes, I'll have a merry Christmas thank you'."

She wished it was over. She felt that tonight would be worse than tomorrow. That was the day itself, but in the hard bright sunlight the gay streamers and tinsel and gaudy trees would look ridiculous, out of place, a little tired and tawdry, and she would be able to jeer a little, to criticise, to think perhaps that after all it was a great fuss about nothing, a mere fraud.

But Christmas Eve was magic. In the soft warm night the lights glowed with memories of childhood Christmasses, of excitement and whispers, giggly secrets, and cooking smells, limp pillowcases lined up by the stairs, visitors coming and going and everyone smiling real smiles and voices crying with real affection, real enjoyment, "Merry Christmas, merry Christmas to you."

Christmas Eve was a cruel time to the lonely. In its jingle of carols came the remembered voices of long ago, reminding that the singers were gone; in the tinsel streamers were the shadow of childish hands, gone too; in the sight of couples, of families, heads together, voices whispering, were memories of dreams and whispers broken like the glass balls on the Christmas trees that were gone now, too.

She had never expected it to be as bad as this. When her mother had died just after last Christmas, she was suddenly no longer "Poor Megan" who had to stay with a bed-ridden old lady. She had never particularly thought of herself as Poor. Her mother's illness hadn't been the unpleasant kind, and the two of them had been friends as well as parent and daughter, and there'd been interests enough in the country town where she'd lived all her life to keep her from feeling cut off from everything.

But suddenly she was no longer even Megan, but Miss Tremont, thirty years old, with her friends married, her mother gone; no one interested in her and no job in the town open to her, and everyone had taken it for granted that now she would head straight for the city and plunge into a new life.

She knew, looking back on it mockingly, that her married friends had secretly envied her. Probably this Christmas, surrounded by their families, harassed, overtired, their minds filled with problems of tomorrow's cooking and tonight's festivities, they thought of her, if they thought about her for even an instant, as spending a night of something the town would have thought of as wild devilment, with cocktails, lobster, nightclubs, dancing till the small hours, and presents galore.

She might have gone back. She'd considered it for a time, then rejected the idea. The town had had no place for her before. It was unlikely that now it would welcome her back. She would be simply a curiosity, an embarrassment, because she was an extra woman alone round festive boards.

So she had stayed, and when the shop closed and she had smiled a last painful smile and spoken a last spuriously gay greeting she would go back to her privacy in Dickson Street.

She had fallen into the trap that waited for those on their own, with her first arrival on the north shore, and her gaining a job in the big newsagents. The people in the store had told her where she might find a flatlette, "nice and private and all to yourself—not like one of those ghastly boarding houses," they had cried.

It was a small private house, and the elderly couple had welcomed her quite pleasantly and had showed her the flatlette at the front of the house, telling her she would be completely private there. She had never realised that privacy was sometimes spelt loneliness. She did her own cleaning. They never entered her bedsitting room, never entered her tiny kitchenette, never invited her into their own section of the house. She might as well have had even the bathroom and laundry to herself. There was a notice on both, setting out her hours of privacy therein. At those hours they were never to be seen. It was almost like sharing the place with two ghosts.

At first she had tried to break down the wall between them—taking a slice of a cake she had made, offering a magazine she had finished with, but her intrusion into their privacy had been met with something approaching suspicion. She had read in their faded eyes, "Is she going to impose on us? We respect her privacy and she should respect ours," and she had shrunk back into her shell.

She should have got away long ago, she thought, beginning to clear up the jumble on the counter. The day had been so busy she'd had no time to clear up as she'd worked. She should have left the job, too. She had thought such a place was sure to get her into conversation with regular customers, let her make friends of a sort, but everyone was in too much of a hurry to more than barely notice she was around. Coins were tossed on the counter and papers and magazines taken; greeting cards were selected in silence. She had tried at first helping with those and had met with suspicion again. She had found that people seemed to resent her questions as to whether the card was for an invalid, a small child or for someone ill. They drew away with a murmured, suspicious, "I can manage, thank you."

Everywhere she seemed to come up against that strange barrier, a clinging to that treasured article, Privacy. She had idly wondered sometimes if the very red-tape-ridden lives of most of them was the cause. There was so much red tape about everything, so many questions and probings, that perhaps no one ever recognised friendliness any more.

Her hands hovered over a spun glass ball. Brilliantly blue like the summer sky over the paddocks at home, it glowed in her hand. I want to go home, she thought suddenly and felt the sandiness of tears under her lashes. I want to be back among people who know that friendly questions are one thing, and probing is another and can tell the difference. I want...

"I want some decorations. Like that ball."

She started. The ball slipped from her fingers and was neatly caught by a pair of strong-fingered male hands, so that her own slim hands, darting after it, fell over the hands and the ball together.

Her cheeks flushed scarlet and she drew sharply back.

"I'm sorry."

"Don't be. It isn't damaged. A beautiful thing. Isn't it?" Leigh held the ball to the light. "I want some like this, but perhaps they'd better be smaller. The tree's a mere babe."

She half smiled. The words hovered on the tip of her tongue, wanting to ask, "Did you buy it for your baby?" then were left unsaid, because of the lesson she'd learned that questions like that veiled eyes, blanked out expressions, brought a mumble in answer.

"There aren't many left, I'm afraid," she said and turned away, stepping onto the ladder, going up, and getting down boxes.

Leigh watched her. A lovely back, he thought wearily. A lovely set of her head on slim shoulders, too. And lovely hair. That cap shape of fairness suited her round solemn face.

But couldn't she smile? Take an interest and pleasure in handling the spun glass ornaments? Perhaps she was tired out, he reflected in sudden compassion, then thought that more likely she simply wanted to close the doors and go. There was probably a man waiting for her somewhere. He glanced at her hands, saw they were ringless, and she was what ... twenty six or seven, or perhaps more, he thought. Difficult to tell with that type of round solemn face and babyish hair. But tonight she'd go off with a man somewhere, dance, have fun, go home to her family, help with younger children perhaps...

He was suddenly bitterly jealous. In perversity, to keep

her away from it for a little longer, he pretended he couldn't make up his mind. Two or three other people came in, breathless, wanting fancy papers and gift ties, and even cards. She served them with a distant politeness, smiling occasionally, returning greetings in a low, soft voice, barely glancing at him, leaving him to his own devices.

He was angry at that. Why couldn't she try to help? He'd never before bought such things. He couldn't visualise the tiny tree decorated out with them.

At last he called, "Couldn't you help me?"

"If you wish." Her clear grey eyes were expressionless, remote. "You said the tree was tiny? These would be the best I think," she touched one box with a finger unadorned with nail varnish. "They're very fragile though." She hesitated, touched the box again, said almost curtly, as though resenting the offer, "I can wrap them up well. If you have to take a bus, there'll be a crowd..."

"No, I don't take a bus." Then, because that sounded curt, he added, "I'm living in Nurrung Court."

"Oh?" She lifted her gaze, gave him a quick speculative glance, then turned away to wrap each ornament in a twist of tissue before closing the box and wrapping that. She handed it to him unsmilingly.

"Thank you. Goodnight. And merry Christmas."

The control that had grown threadbare throughout the day finally snapped. She said, and her voice jeered mockery at the words, "Oh yes, a merry, merry Christmas."

He turned. For an instant they stood, motionless, staring at one another.

Another, he thought. Another who'll be alone tonight. Dear god, why? He took a step back towards her, then a crowd of children came running in, thrusting him aside. He went on hesitating a moment, but two other people were crowding in. The place was filled and he had to go.

And after all, what could he have done? He asked himself that as he walked briskly back to the Court. You can't say to a woman, "You're another! One of the ones who can't bear tonight!"

She would have clammed up, told him to leave the place, ignoring him if he wouldn't go.

Life, and humanity in particular, was stark, raving mad, he thought in weary disgust.

. . .

Virginia knew she wasn't particularly good at telling the time, but she knew enough of clock faces to know that it was growing incredibly late. It must, she thought in something approaching panic, be hours—quite hours—since Miss Tarks had gone out with the man, after saying it was a game.

But a game didn't last this long. It didn't go right beyond your bedtime, for hours and hours. It didn't leave you in silence, wondering, getting frightened. Surely Miss Tarks must know her visitor would get frightened, locked in and not knowing what was happening at all, or when the woman was coming back? Miss Tarks must know it...

She stood there miserably, chewing on the knuckle of her thumb. Was Miss Tarks deliberately giving her a good hard fright? As punishment? Had she known about that bowl breaking? Lady Helps had eyes in the backs of their head, Virginia was quite aware. So ... had Miss Tarks known and locked the door and gone out deliberately and left her guest to get more and more frightened?

It wasn't impossible. She'd known one housekeeper who'd done exactly that—locked her up and gone out for five solid hours. Virginia had been weeping from fright when she'd been released and the woman had nodded in grim satisfaction. "That'll teach you, miss. You get under my feet and I'll lock you up and leave you to stew and you won't even know if I'll ever come back at all. I might walk right out and then you won't get out till your dad comes home in the night, or next day if he's travelling overnight. You think that out, miss, and remember it."

Virginia began to shake, then started to giggle in relief, remembering Miss Tarks wasn't a housekeeper. Oh, the relief of remembering that! Miss Tarks lived in this place. She couldn't just walk out for a whole night. She'd be home soon.

And why, if she was doing this as punishment, hadn't she said, grimly, "Virginia, I *know* about that crystal bowl. I'm locking you in, and leaving you to think things out. When I come back I'll expect a real apology." Why not that? She was used to that sort of thing, so why say to her,"Hush, it's a game. Hide. It's a secret," leaving her to think something nice and Christmassy was coming?

Nothing made sense.

She went slowly back to the window. The nice man who'd waved to her was gone. He'd turned out his light, too, so she couldn't see his dear little tree any more. She leaned out hopefully, looking for other faces, other waving hands, but the lighted windows were curtained, blank. Only right away down in the court, by the big decorated tree there, was a human figure.

Hopefully she waved.

. . .

It was beautiful. Really beautiful. Made you feel like a boy again, with all the Christmas fun bubbling up inside you like a fizzy drink in a bottle, waiting for the big moment when the cork popped out on the real excitement and the presents were unwrapped and the pudding brought in and for once in your year you could make a downright pig of yourself without a word of rebuke. He chuckled at the thought, then looked round guiltily, thankful the place was deserted. He was getting real bad at talking and laughing away to himself, he thought with the gaiety and laughter suddenly gone. If he wasn't careful the authorities would be bundling him up and tucking him into some hospital corner with a note over his bed, "Rodney Leaderbee, aged seventy nine, Senile".

That'd be lovely and he wouldn't put it past them. That young doctor had looked at him queerly the other day. Had as good as told him he was past looking after himself properly just because he'd got sore feet. He'd admitted that getting his bones to bend so he could get down to drying his feet was difficult and had agreed equably enough that wet feet at his age didn't do any good, but that didn't mean he needed to be shuttled into a home. He'd said with dignity, "I'll get my darters to see to it," and had added as a further whopping lie, "I've got six darters, see, and I bet that's more than you've been able to produce, young fellow, legal or otherwise."

The little whipper-snapper had turned beet red. He got a real laugh out of remembering that, and repeating the conversation over and over to himself, dwelling on the bit where he'd claimed, "I've got six darters," as cool as anyone pleased.

He wasn't going to let any little whipper-snapper pry into his affairs, and find there wasn't even a single daughter or son or anyone else. That would have meant the authorities round, harassing him. The landlord would have jumped on the waggon too. He'd tried often enough to get his tenant out of the neat weatherboard cottage. They'd have bundled him off right enough, he thought grimly. A nice sort of Christmas present that would have been for a man.

Abruptly a long shuddering sigh went through his still portly body, and his red veined cheeks seemed to fall in a little with his indrawn breath. The little dark eyes screwed up in a pain that hadn't anything to do with his rheumatism and sore feet and bent back. It was purely mental pain, at the thought that even that sort of Christmas present might have proved better than none; that in a home there'd at least have been turkey and a piping hot pudding and a Christmas tree.

His pension hadn't run to buying a tree and trimmings. In fact it hadn't run to anything much, but turkeys and piping hot puddings were out in any case. These days his hands trembled so much he found it dangerous to try and cook because he couldn't handle the pots and pans properly. That meant living out of tins. That was wickedly expensive, he remembered sadly. There'd been no chance all year to save for a tree.

Which was why he'd come to the Court, to admire the one in the courtyard there. He'd come every evening since the tree was brought in and tubbed there and decorated up with lights and trimmings. It was a far better tree than he'd ever possessed himself. The most beautiful one he'd ever seen in fact. Which made it all the more strange and peculiar and terrible that no one else but himself ever seemed to come and gaze.

Sitting there in the courtyard of an evening he saw the home unit owners coming and going and their visitors too, but he'd never seen one of them stop and stare and sit down and really take it in and think and remember all the Christmas fun they'd once had.

Perhaps, he thought acutely, they didn't need to. It was only when you were old and there was no more fun at all that you had to sit down and think and remember; when you feasted in memory and not in reality.

He lifted his head, turning slowly to gaze up at the tower building. He admired it, while disliking it. It was a proud thing and a marvellous creation and it had fancy brickwork and a lot of glass and smart tiles on the roof, but there was something about it like a rabbit warren. There was nothing personal about it, like there was about a row of cottages. Even the blinds were all the same so that at night, like now, you were faced with a stretch of lighted windows, all covered in the same way.

Only one window . . . he smiled. Well that was a treat. He hadn't known there was a child in the building. Perhaps she was a visitor, leaning out to admire the tree, and wave. To himself he realised.

Warmth and gladness touched him. The small fluttering hand from so far up the brick sides of the building was almost as good as the touch of small fingers in his thickly veined trembling hands.

He lifted a shaky arm and waved back, lifting his head, smiling, but slowly the smile died. Anxiety took its place. She was leaning too far out, he thought anxiously. Or he was. At that distance, with the figure a mere outline against a lighted room, he couldn't for sure tell if it was a girl or boy.

He rose and went shakily round the building, seeking the button he had seen once, marked Caretaker. He had to wait some time and then the middle aged man who opened the door looked cranky. He stood with shirtsleeves rolled up, hands on heavy hips, barking, "Well?"

Leaderbee sighed. He wished people these days weren't always in such a hurry, and so curt. He said heavily, "There's a little child up there. Leaning out too far if you were to ask me. Waving to passers-by. Having a game, you know. It shouldn't be allowed. Not leaning out like that. There could be..."

The younger man sounded really bad tempered now, snapping out, "I'm not a kid's nurse!" Then he heaved a sigh. "O.K. old-timer, where is it? Let's have a look." He paced beside the older man into the court and stood staring up, counting, lips moving as he muttered, "Wallaces there, and that's Roper—and that's ... yes..." he gave a triumphant smack of one hand on the other, "Tarks! That's Miss Tarks and the Segal kid. That's the Segal kid up there. Father's away, see. Got no mother. She's a holy terror. You take it from me. If she fell she'd bounce up and walk off. Devil looks after his own, and only the good die young, see. Oh, she's a terror that one. They've had a procession of women coming and going in two shakes in that place. Can't stand the kid. I've had it from them all." He shook his head. "Don't you worry about her, old-timer. Miss Tarks will have an eye on her, you can count on that. She won't let her lean out too far before she tans her sit-down."

He went striding away, not looking back. Leaderbee went on standing there. As he watched, the child moved backwards. Called back, he thought comfortably. Oh yes, she'd be fine if there was a woman up there. He needn't worry. He moved back to sit by the tree again, thinking, remembering.

CHAPTER SEVEN

It was the same story everywhere. He should have realised it, Aldan knew. His face didn't change expression as for the tenth time that night a desk clerk said briskly, "Sorry, sir, we're booked right out right over the holiday season. Very sorry, sir."

"No room at the inn, eh?" he said tiredly, bending again to pick up the case that was now bereft of the traveller's cheques.

The clerk smiled distantly, turning away. Aldan went out into the Christmas lights of the street again, and simply stood there. He was so tired he couldn't think beyond getting shelter for the night, and a chance to sleep and clear the muddle from his head, so he could plan out what to do for the best.

He'd managed to change the flight ticket for the following evening. Whether he would be on the plane he simply didn't know. He thought he would be. He'd feel safer with the stretch of sea between himself and the police—it was an illusion, he knew, but he didn't care. New Zealand was better than simply going interstate, because he had plotted, over the months, how he would live there, gaining information of towns, of jobs. Interstate, even the city in which he stood, hadn't been plotted over. If he stayed he'd have to start searching for a job and somewhere to live and soon—for all he knew, right now—Isobel was . . .

He thought suddenly, I've got to keep an eye on the place till I get that plane. I have to make sure there isn't a sudden commotion or the arrival of the police. I have to watch it. If she's found I can't go back to the airport. Greta might have tipped them off to Herbert Baring, his appearance, all about him, by the time I get back.

He was appalled that he hadn't thought of that point

before. He went on standing, jostled a little by passing crowds, not caring about it, thinking only of the lighted tower building and the street with the harbour beyond and ... yes, he realised, a private hotel. He was sure there'd been one he'd seen. If he could get a room there—and surely out of the centre of the city there'd be vacancies even tonight—he could watch Nurrung Court easily enough.

Because money was precious he didn't hail a taxi. He went by the ferry, sitting outside, among the young lovers. They resented his silent solitary figure smoking out there, he knew, but didn't care, and the trip was only short. It was still only ten thirty when he pressed his thumb against the bell of the Merton Private Hotel, and only a few minutes after when he entered the hall to be shown up a narrow stairway and into a cubbyhole of a room at the back of the place.

He was wildly resentful that the only window showed him not the entrance of Nurrung Court, but the back courtyard of the place, but it couldn't be helped. He paid for the room, as demanded, shut the door behind the woman who'd shown him up and went back to the window, trying to work out if he could see Isobel's windows.

From the lift he'd turned right, he remembered. That meant the right arm of the courtyard, and he smiled for the first time that evening because he could see the whole length of the arm. And the whole sixth floor of the arm. He pinpointed that, telling himself that after all not being able to see the front entrance didn't matter. If a commotion began it would be centred in Isobel's flat. He'd know, soon after the police cars arrived at the front of the building, because lights would flare on in Isobel's windows.

He'd turned off the light as he'd gone out, he remembered, remembering too that three of her windows had overlooked the court—the living room, the kitchen and one of the bedrooms.

His gaze raked along the sixth floor. He frowned in disbelief when he couldn't find three darkened windows together. He could pinpoint two, with lighted ones each side, but not three. Not in the whole stretch.

Maybe, he pondered, it was the left arm of the courtyard he needed, after all. He felt so tired he couldn't think properly, but he was sure he'd gone right, and he remembered quite positively snapping off the light in the living room, so there should be three windows...

He blinked. He remembered in sharp awareness going into the lighted kitchen. Isobel had gone in afterwards, but had she switched off the light or not? He didn't know, but searching the windows again, he was certain that she hadn't. So her flat was where the two dark windows together showed in the long line of light.

For a moment he was panic stricken, then laughed at himself. Who was going to comment on a kitchen window light burning all night at this time of the year? And in daytime? What about that, he pondered, then shook his head. It mightn't even show up in strong daylight. If it did, why should anyone worry?

He remembered, with real amusement now, that people often left lights burning in one room of the house, if they meant to be away a couple of nights, so at night no one would be tempted by an apparently empty place.

He shook his head. So long as a commotion didn't start, so long as windows didn't open and heads crane out, peering up at those three windows he'd pinpointed, he was all right. He'd sleep and watch, and sit and watch through Christmas day, and if it was all right, and he'd planned out his way ahead successfully again, he'd go back to the plane tomorrow night and fly out.

. . .

"Peace on earth, goodwill to men..." the canned music jangled out from the record shop on the other corner as Megan came out into the night. "Peace on earth, goodwill, goodwill..."

The whole block of shop doors were closed now. Only the voice on the record and the animated Santa Claus who perpetually worked in his workshop tableaux in the window of another store, and the tinsel ribbons and streamers and decorated packages in other windows remained of the hustle and bustle of the past few days. When the doors opened again the windows would be stripped and the music silenced. For the moment, in flats behind and above the shops, families were busy on private celebrations.

She walked slowly away, to the end of the shops, stepping into darkness pierced only by street lights, canyoned on either side by lighted windows. She had the long length of pavement all to herself and a lean streak of ginger cat. Even he didn't want her company. His eyes flickered green disapproval of her outstretched, coaxing hand.

Probably on his way to his girlfriend, she thought in wry amusement. They'd dance in the moonlight later on and sing their own carols to the midnight sky. The thought made her laugh as she turned the corner. She remembered the man then and her hands touching his, feeling the warmth of them, and the strength.

Nurrung Court, lighted up so it looked for all the world like a man-made Christmas tree of brick, was facing her at the bottom of the street, blocking out the harbour from view.

Walking towards it, remembering the man, the blue glass ball, the warm strong hands, she wondered if the baby tree was decorated now, perhaps placed by a baby's cot in some trim little nursery. He was possibly now sitting facing a pretty young woman, wrapping the last of their presents, filling the baby's small sock, talking of tomorrow—or maybe he was throwing a party.

In that moment she knew that if she had known his name, and the number of his flat, she would have walked in through the wide glass doors of the Court, gone across the carpeted foyer and found the flat and rung and knocked and made some excuse—something about charging him the wrong price for the glass balls perhaps—just so she could have seen the tree, perhaps been asked to share a drink, a toast to the season and the coming year, maybe even asked to share in the talk. Just for fifteen minutes, half an hour . . .

She was glad there was no hope of it, glad she had no

chance to make such a fool of herself, because he might have read too much in her eyes. She remembered the way she had mocked his greeting, the way he had turned and stared, as though knowing just how she felt, knowing and recognising her for what she was—an outsider, one who'd be alone tonight.

She'd walk to the nature strip along the harbour wall she told herself. You were called a fool if you were a woman and walked in quiet places like that at night, alone, but tonight she didn't care, and there was no violence in the world she was sure. Loneliness, yes, but nothing worse tonight.

The stars were brighter now than anything man had fashioned in spun glass and tinsel for his Christmas trees. She smiled at them, at the lights on the harbour as the ferries crossed, at the lights of the city itself across the water, then she turned.

She drew in her breath, instantly, completely, lost in memories. How beautiful it was! All the imagined trees of childhood come to reality. She was suddenly furiously angry that she had never bothered before to walk down so far, to realise the back of the Court lived up to its name and had a real courtyard, and that in it now was a Christmas tree straight out of fairy-tales.

Slowly she walked towards it, going up the flight of steps to the footpath, entering the courtyard to stand gazing up at the lighted windows, letting her gaze fall slowly from the glittering crown of the tree to its base.

A slow flush began in her cheeks then, rose to her forehead and died away. She shifted in embarrassment, turning sharply, aware of the watching eyes, wondering if the light from windows had spilled onto her face and knowing that it must have revealed too much and hating the fact that someone should have seen her in such an unguarded moment.

Then the voice said, "Ah no, don't run away. I won't hurt you, you know, miss. Heavens above, I'm seventy nine! Long past chasing young ladies in the dark!"

She swung round again, stifling a laugh.

She said lightly, "I didn't expect to be chased, but I've no business here. I thought ... I might be disturbing you. I'm trespassing I suppose."

"If you are, I must be, too. I've come round every night since they put it up and no one's chased me off yet. They'd expect people to come and stand and stare and sit and think and just admire it. Wouldn't they?"

"Yes." She walked slowly up to the seat and he moved to make room for her. "But tonight everyone would be too busy. I suppose, other nights..."

She fell silent, thinking of groups parading here, couples with linked arms, children gazing in awe. Why hadn't she known about it, so she could have joined in the throng? Spoken to people and been spoken to in turn?

But he was telling her, "There's never anyone else here. I expect them..." he gestured to the lighted windows, "the folks who own those home units, have their own trees inside, see. And outsiders, except you and me, don't like to trespass."

She remembered the baby tree, the man's careful selection of baubles for it. She cried out, "But there are children here! *They* must come..."

"There's only one I've ever seen and that's tonight. She leaned out the window up there and waved to me." His shaky voice held sudden disapproval, "they ought to've put her to bed long ago, but she's still up. I've been sitting here looking. A while back she started in waving to a fellow *that* side. He was sitting in *his* window, with the blinds up, decorating a little bit of a tree, and they were waving back and forth and having a real game. She ought to've been in bed though." His veined cheeks caved in with inhaled breath that seemed to go on and on and was released again in a breath so slight it made her wonder if his body was so old, so poorly conditioned now to living, that it held grimly to all the air he drew in, fighting against losing it again.

She asked, "Won't your family be worrying about *you* being out at this hour?" and her gaze was suddenly appraising the shabby suit and frayed shirt collar.

He jerked, and she saw in his dark little eyes, in the light from the windows, the wariness and withdrawal and suspicion.

He said with dignity, "It's a fine night. And there's such a lot doing at home. At ... with my darters you see. Six of them. Six darters," he straightened his bent back, looking at her levelly and added wings to his imagination. "In a bit I'll have to get back and get dressed up. To play Santa, you see. For my grandarters, that is."

He wondered how many he might claim, then saw again the small fluttering hand. He cried out, "There, look! See, they haven't put her ... or is it a boy? ... to bed yet. There, look, you can see the child waving. And look over there," he touched her arm excitedly, "there's the chap. See? Having a regular game." He watched with her for a couple of seconds in silence, then said, rather forlornly, "She was waving to me first, before he put up his blind that way and started in trimming his tree."

"You know," he gave her slim hand a little tap with one bent finger, "I'd say he was alone tonight. Like me." He was quite unaware he'd given himself away, "And he's sat there trimming the tree and keeping her waving just to give himself a companion, like. Being alone tonight ... that's bad, that's ..." his voice rose. "There, look, she's seen us! Come on, now lass, wave away!"

She started to laugh. How absurd, yet how strangely comforting, was the game—four hands fluttering in friendliness to one another. The man had seen them too and was waving to them as well as to the child now. She could see him only as an outline, and the tree was so small that ...

Small ... a baby tree ...

She wondered then if it was the man whose hands she had touched—if that fluttering hand was one that had caught at a ball whose blue had reminded her of summer skies over the paddocks of her childhood—if he'd come at the last minute that way so he could trim his tree and keep the child watching, so that tonight he wasn't totally alone.

On impulse she turned, "Look, if you're alone tonight alone for Christmas ..."

She saw the suspicion dart into his little eyes. His red veined cheeks seem to puff out and collapse again in a sharply indrawn breath. He drew his bent back straight and stood up, "You have that wrong, miss. Didn't I tell you about my darters? I've got to go now. Got to dress up to play Santa you see. For my grandarters, that is."

He went hurrying, muttering a little to himself in anxiety, wondering who she was. She'd have meant to be kind, but she'd have pried, he was certain, and perhaps whispered to the authorities about him and his being alone and wandering around at night, waving to children...

He was frightened now. People were funny sometimes if you took an interest in their kids—girls, especially. They didn't understand about you being lonely. They just whispered things like Senile, and Nasty Old Man, and next thing...

He sighed, then set his lips firmly together. He wasn't going to think about it. The girl wouldn't be around tomorrow. She'd be with her family, of course. So he needn't worry. He'd do just what he'd planned. He'd make up a pile of sandwiches and cut himself a big wedge of the cake he'd bought himself and bring the lot to the court. He was going —his eyes brightened at the thought—to sit under the tree and have a Christmas party for himself and it.

. . .

Virginia was tired. Her eyes kept wanting to close, but she wouldn't let them. She was frightened and had already cried twice. She had cried all the time she had clambered on a chair and been forced to use the sink as a lavatory. The shame of that, and the terror that Miss Tarks was lurking somewhere and could see her and was about to pounce on her and whip her for it, made her feel violently ill.

But still the woman hadn't come back and the door was still locked and the room beyond the keyhole was as dark as ever.

There had been relief for a while when she had gone back to the window and seen the man across the court. He had waved to her and started to trim his little tree. She wished she could have been closer, wished the court wasn't so wide, so she could have called to him and told him about Miss Tarks and asked him what she should do. She would have been able to see the tree and the decorations better, too—they were merely a blur at that distance. But it was fun watching and waving.

Once she had thought of the phone. She didn't know about them. There wasn't one in the Segal flat and no one had ever shown her how to use one, but she knew you could lift the receiver and speak to people if you dialled a number. The trouble was she didn't know any numbers and she had searched the whole kitchen without finding a directory. She had vaguely remembered that once a phone box had been out of order and her father had spoken to someone called the Operator. She had experimented by lifting the receiver and saying carefully, clearly, "Operator, please come and open the door for me," but nothing at all happened, and finally she drifted back to the window.

The man came back almost at once and waved to her. Then she saw two figures down in the courtyard by the tree. In a minute all of them were waving—herself and the man, and the pair below and she was laughing in excitement, because it was like playing puppets—you lifted your hand and obediently all the little puppet figures lifted theirs too.

She wanted it to go on, for them not to go away and leave her alone again, but abruptly one figure below moved off, quickly, and then the other followed, not even gazing back.

Finally the man went from his window, too.

. . .

He was going to ring up, Leigh told himself. He was going to ring the child and speak to her and wish her a merry Christmas and ask her what she hoped she'd find in her stocking in the morning.

He remembered Robbins talking about the child having no mother and the father being away but now, impatient with his forgetfulness, he couldn't remember the name of the woman who owned the unit across the court.

Cole? Something to do with coal, he wondered, then thought, No, Tar. That was it. Tar-something.

He remembered then and went to the directory, but his finger remained still on the page.

He sighed. *Miss* Tarks. If she could afford to buy a unit in the Court she was probably an elderly spinster of private means—definitely not the sort of person who'd invite a stranger who called on the phone and told her he was alone and wanted to chat to the child, to come up to her home for a drink and a talk. She probably wouldn't so much as let him speak to the child at all, he reflected. After all it was going to sound a bit odd to say, "Look, Miss Tarks, I've been waving to the little girl across the court all evening. I trimmed a tree just for her because I'm lonely and tonight of all nights that's hell and more. I want to hear a human voice, share someone's Christmas pleasure and delight..."

He gave a jerk of laughter. He'd been mad to think of it. Act like that, ring at all and even ask the child's name, he told himself, and she'd probably ring straight down to the caretaker and complain about him.

He grimaced, remembering the man talking about her—saying she valued things above people any day. Certainly not the type who'd take pity on a lonely man, even on Christmas Eve.

Dispiritedly he thrust the directory back on to the shelf. He went back to the window, but the lighted window across the courtyard was empty again. In sudden anger against human conventions and human suspicion that could make cause for complaint in him waving to a child across the court, he shot down the blinds, got out his briefcase, and settled down to work.

CHAPTER EIGHT

They were all the same now, all secretive and shaded against her gaze. Slow tears welled in her eyes again. Why had the man pulled down his blind and gone, she wondered unhappily.

And where was Miss Tarks?

There wasn't a sound in the flat, though she could hear radios playing. Carols mostly, the sound floating through the open windows all round the court. It seemed absurd there were dozens and dozens, hundreds even, of people only a little way away and yet she was all alone.

She wondered suddenly if Miss Tarks could see her, and she shrank back, peering closely at each shadow, half expecting to see a corner of a blind tweaked back and a sharp suspicious eye put to the space. She thought it quite possible that Miss Tarks had gone into another flat, leaving her visitor to get frightened and terrified, to punish her. She'd sit in one of the other places and sip a drink and eat a slice of home-made Christmas cake, and think all the time how her guest—her wicked guest who had broken the crystal bowl—was being punished and she'd smile—a pursed-lip secret little smile of satisfaction.

It wouldn't matter to her that later on Virginia's father would be angry—when he'd heard about it all. She wouldn't mind. She'd just say slyly, like all of them—housekeepers, and daily women and Lady Helps—"Well if you prefer to believe Virginia, Mr. Segal, rather than me, it's best you find someone else to look after her. Isn't that so? After all I can find plenty of other jobs any day of the week—why people are falling over themselves to get a decent woman to give a little help, so I'll just..."

But no, she remembered, Miss Tarks wouldn't say that. She wasn't being paid for this Christmas. She was doing a

Favour. Her father had impressed that on Virginia, "She's doing us a big Favour, Ginny," he'd pleaded earnestly, "so you be good as gold, huh? How big a Favour it is I don't think you can begin to realise."

She hadn't, but she realised enough now to know that Miss Tarks wouldn't care a jot what Arthur Segal said about his daughter being frightened so badly. She'd probably just laugh, or say slyly, with satisfaction, "Well at least, Mr. Segal, you won't be pestering me to grant you Favours any more, will you?"

And then ... Virginia sighed ... she'd mention the glass bowl ... and the accident.

Accident, she thought, dwelling on the word, suddenly completely terrified. Had Miss Tarks met with an accident? Had she gone downstairs with her visitor to see him off and slipped or been hit by a car or ... oh a thousand things could have happened she realised. In imagination she could see a big white ambulance come rushing along the road, to stop and scoop up Miss Tarks and carry her away—Miss Tarks with her neat dark hair all disordered, and her mouth wide open and her eyes closed.

She ran to the living room door, trying to force the handle to move freely and release her. When it wouldn't she pounded on the door itself, crying, till her hands were sore. When she stopped beating the tears had dried on her face and she was calmer, conscious now of louder sounds than previously. Sounds right next door she realised—right the other side of the kitchen wall, in the flat next door. Loud sounds. Music and two loud bangs and what seemed like yells and cries of laughter.

She ran to the wall and hit at that, but her small hands seemed powerless to make much noise. She went to the cupboard then, got out the broom and began to bang, as the noise next door increased, thrusting the broom handle as hard as she could against the wall.

. . .

Margot Hickens gave a shriek of laughter as the champagne cork came out with explosive force. She knew she had had too much to drink already—first at the office party, then at the hotel where a group of them had rushed off for a final drink that had turned into several. Then Rog had met her at the door of the flat with another filled glass, and now the crowd had arrived.

My god, my god, my head, she thought confusedly, while her mouth went on smiling and she was mentally ticking up the frightening cost of the drinks being poured, and even spilled—she noted one overturned glass and was furiously angry, while she still smiled. Add the grog to the cost of tomorrow's turkey and all the gifts for the office crowd, she thought bitterly, and it was sheer murder.

Merry Christmas! Merry headache more likely. She hated the crowd, she hated Christmas, she hated her job and her dyed hair and her carefully made up face that tried to preserve the looks of forty when she was fifty three. Most of all she hated the home unit. What on earth, she wondered, chattering on brightly and smiling endlessly, had made her and Rog think it would be heaven on earth and sign up for it with payments that meant her dyeing her hair and dieting and going back into the rat-race of office work to help cover expenses?

It had been a headache from the word go—none of their old furniture had fitted, there seemed no room for hobbies and what with complaints...

Her mouth stayed open, silently, in mid sentence, then slowly closed while her hands clenched tightly.

The nerve of her! Not eleven o'clock even! And Christmas Eve when parties were going on all over the place. Anyway they weren't making that much noise. The radio was on, certainly and there was talk and laughter and a few yells but to pound away like that...

She went quickly, ignoring the person she'd been talking to, into the living room. She caught Rog's eye, gave a jerk of her head and when he'd followed her into the kitchen she jerked her head again, towards the other wall, towards the noise.

All of the crowd in the room were silent now, all staring towards the wall. Margot gave a sudden jerk of laughter. "That friends, is our dear neighbour. Every time we blow our nose she rings to say we're ruining her health with noise."

Rog was angry. She could tell that. He couldn't find any amusement in the pounding. He said, "The damned old cat! You'd think on Christmas Eve..."

She said, with a sudden gust of compassion fighting with the last drink that was niggling at her temper, "She's probably alone in there. She's probably jealous as hell of us. That's why."

He was heading for the hall where their phone was. She ran after him, clutching at his arm, knowing in dismay that he'd had so much to drink that he wasn't going to listen to her—he was simply going to let his temper take over. "Rog," she tried to stop him, "she's lonely. Ask her in for a drink. Poor old thing, she's..."

"She's younger than you!" he told her brutally. "And she's a damned old basket. She's complained from the day we moved in and this is the end. What does she think we are— a bunch of kids to shut up as teacher demands? She can take the party and like it!"

He was finding the number, dialling, while she stood there helplessly.

. . .

Out of sheer exhaustion Virginia had stopped banging on the wall. She sat down limply, wondering what would happen now. The people next door must know that something was wrong. She wondered what they'd do first. Ring the caretaker perhaps? She didn't like that idea much. He knew she, Virginia, was up here, and he didn't like her. He might say it wasn't his business. He was fond of saying that. He kept saying it when her father had complained about her being locked out of the Segal flat one time. He'd said, "You should have used your master key, Robbins, and let her inside again."

Robbins hadn't been impressed by that argument. He'd given back, "Listen Mr. Segal, you think of this—I let her in and there's no one there say—your Daily having hopped off to the shops and what happens? That little terror gets up to something and hurts herself. Who gets the blame? Me. Al Robbins. *I* get the blame for letting her back in. I won't be a party to it."

She could count out Mr. Robbins helping, she thought in disgust. But the people next door would know something was wrong and they'd try and do something. She wasn't sure what. Maybe get the master key off Robbins and come on in. But perhaps they'd talk a while first. She moved restlessly, eyeing the phone, wishing she could ring them and tell them to hurry and come and let her out.

If only the directory had been there she was sure she could have read enough of it to learn how to manage the phone, but this one was only an extension and she was remembering now that the other phone and the directory were in the hall on a neat little stand.

When the phone rang, calling to her, she gave a cry of delight, running to it, cradling the receiver against her ear and pushing back the veil of fine hair so it wouldn't get in the road. She wasn't prepared for the blast of sound that made her jerk backwards, at the angry voice that soared out into her ear, "Listen lady, you just stop that! Stop it, I tell you. It won't do you a scrap of good. If *I* like it this party's going on to dawn!"

There was a sharp click and silence. She gulped, said into the mouthpiece indignantly, "But I'm locked in. Please come and let me out," but there was no answer. She went on and on, but still the phone was silent and in a little while all the noise began again next door, while the phone refused to speak to her.

She let the receiver fall, dangling at the end of the cord, and went back to the broom, picking it up, as the noise swelled up and up, ignoring her. She began to pound, violently, hysteria welling up in her small body.

. . .

Next door Margot said disgustedly, "For pity's sake! Is she cuckoo! Rog..."

He went into the other room, came back with the portable radiogram, put on a record and turned it on full blast, putting the instrument right against the wall. The blast of sound pounded out, filling the small room. Margot winced, the others clapped hands to ears. Rog said tightly, 'She asked for it. She'll get it. I'm going to leave that going till the party's over. Come on into the other room and shut off the dividing doors. Bring the food, Margot. And the grog. We'll only come in again for ice and for putting on the record when that one's done.

. . .

Robbins lifted the receiver, listened, rolled the name over in his mind and yawned. Welch, he thought. Yes, they were two who'd known he was down in the basement. But they hadn't tipped him. They had, he remembered again, looked faintly outraged he'd even popped out of his basement and landed on their doorstep with a smile and Merry Christmas.

He said disgustedly, "Yeah?" listened again, thought, then said, "Bangings. And a radiogram. It's Christmas Eve, y'know. Ah?" His expression brightened. A slow grin crossed his face. That'd be the Hickens pair he reflected, amusement growing. Friends in nearly every Saturday night and plenty of drink according to the bottles that had to be disposed of next day. So the Hickens were giving a noisy party, with Miss Tarks stuck next door. He wondered if she'd soon be on the phone too, though last time he'd told her flat that he couldn't do a thing—that the Hickens were entitled to any party they liked.

The thought of her banging and banging away at them just made him laugh.

He said, "Look, Mr. Welch, there's nothing *I* can do. Those people've bought a home unit just like you and Mrs. Welch. They're entitled to one noisy party a year. This *is* Christmas Eve y'know. Look, whyn't you pop on up and introduce yourselves to them and have a drink."

He pulled a face at the answer, listened again, snorted in sudden amusement and said, "The banging? Oh that's Santa Claus getting down the chimney. Didn't you know that?" and banged the receiver back on its rest.

Laughter shook him. It must be a riot up there, he reflected. Miss Tarks banging away and doing her block in a temper and the Hickens in a temper making more and more noise to drown her out. Oh lord, she'd be in a paddy. He sucked in his lips appreciatively, faintly sorry now for the child. The old cow would take it out on the kid for a certainty in the morning. Especially when she found out about the broken bowl.

"Oh my word," he said aloud, "you'll catch it, miss."

CHAPTER NINE

He got up again from the surprisingly comfortable easy chair and went back to the window. Nurrung Court wasn't so brightly lighted up now. There were long stretches of darkened windows where before there had been lights. His gaze flickered over the building, counted, picked up the windows he was interested in and concentrated there.

He stared, unbelievingly.

It was wrong, quite wrong. He must have been wrong all along about those windows being Isobel's. He had to be! He began desperately counting again, making sure it was really the sixth floor, knowing it was, even while he counted, knowing quite definitely that from the lift he'd turned right and that he was now looking at the right arm of the building.

But where there had been two dark windows together there were now three. Three dark windows in a row, and there'd been three windows overlooking the court from Isobel's flat. He'd looked through them. The kitchen one, the living room one and one of the bedrooms. Three windows in a row. Frantically he began searching along the line of windows. There was only one other darkened window in that row. Right at the end near the harbour.

The three dark ones had to be Isobel's, but there'd been a light before, in one. In the one he'd pinpointed as the kitchen.

But there wasn't anyone there to run and turn off a burning light.

Sick waves of panic were muddling his thoughts, making him incapable of thinking straight. It was quite impossible someone had turned off the light, unless ... but if someone had gone in, why wasn't there a commotion, windows opening, blinds going up, heads craning out to see what was going on?

He thought desperately, It's at the front. I should have been watching the front! There'll be police cars there. They'll be quiet, trying not to be seen, trying not to cause any upset at all. They'll want to get her out, and search the place, catch people unawares and question them. They'll want...

Me. They'll want *me*, thought mocked. They'll be looking for me right now and when Greta knows she'll tell them about the plane ticket and they'll be there waiting...

Sanity came back slowly.

He started to shake with sheer relief, sitting there sweating while calmness came back. If they'd found her the flat wouldn't now be in darkness. There would have been lights in all the rooms. They'd be searching the place, photographing, looking for fingerprints, all the things they did when violence had happened.

So he was quite wrong. She hadn't been found. He must have made some sort of mistake about the location of her flat. But if those windows weren't hers, which were? He stood there wretchedly, looking along them. He couldn't pick out three dark ones together, or even two dark ones together anywhere in that side of the building. Not anywhere that could count as the sixth floor. Even if you thought the floors might be numbered first and on, without any ground floor, which was how he'd counted in the first place, there were still no windows that fitted in.

It wasn't possible. But it wasn't possible either that someone could have gone in and found her and simply turned off the lights and run away without a word.

Turning and twisting, his mind closed on the thought it was all a trap, that they knew about him, that Greta had followed him here and told the police where he was, in case he ran, and that they'd found Isobel. Perhaps they'd wondered at him coming here with Isobel right opposite and they'd gone to warn her. Anyway they'd found her, and deliberately, knowing he was watching, they'd switched off that light, knowing he'd see and sit there sweating and wondering till the time came when he had to go and find out...

They'd get him easily then. There'd be no possibility of him having another gun and fighting it out if they came over here to take him. No indeed. They were luring him, he thought in panic. Luring him over.

He didn't stop to think how crazily absurd it all was. He told himself cunningly he was smarter than they were. They might be in darkness, waiting, but they wouldn't ignore a phone call. If they were there they'd lift the receiver and speak. Then he'd know.

He went running out, letting the door bang behind him. He ran downstairs to the pay phone in the hall, juggling with coins, dialling the number he knew—as he knew everything else about Isobel, memorizing it all over the long months of waiting.

There was only the engaged signal. He listened to it, knowing only irritation now, irritation against Isobel.

It was her all over, he thought disgustedly. She kept taking the receiver off the hook, though he kept telling her the p.m.g. didn't like it and anyway someone could ring about something important and they wouldn't even know. She'd just laughed at him and she always said the p.m.g. could go and jump in the lake and what did he think was going to happen? That they were going to win the lottery?

He'd tell her...

He remembered then with a sense of searing shock, why he was ringing and that Isobel was dead.

Slowly he put the receiver down. It wasn't the police. It was Isobel all over, all right, in leaving the receiver off the hook, but if the police had come they wouldn't have left it that way. The phone would have rung in the darkened flat, and they'd have answered it.

But the light had gone off.

Anxiously he went back to his room, going back to the window, beginning to count the floors again, looking at the windows and speculating, looking at the lighted Christmas tree in the courtyard.

Then he gasped. He started to laugh, long shaky breaths of relief.

That was it. The light in the kitchen had simply burned out in the globe. That was all. Just as the globe in one of the Christmas tree lights had burned out and darkened as he'd watched.

It was all right. Quite all right. The best thing that could have happened. No one now was going to remark a light burning in daylight. The light had simply burnt out and Isobel was in darkness.

"Goodnight, Is," he mocked to the three darkened windows, and started to prepare for bed.

CHAPTER TEN

Virginia woke all at once. It had been the same way she had gone to sleep—all in a moment. She had turned off the light, after eating a biscuit and drinking some milk and carefully tidying up so there'd be no cause for complaint later on. Then she had curled up on the padded bench seat of the breakfast nook and had hardly finished getting herself into a comfortable position before she was asleep.

Now she was instantly awake, remembering.

Uncurling her small body, she smoothed back her disordered veil of fair tangled hair as best she could, quite sure, absolutely positive, that in the night Miss Tarks had come sneaking back, had seen her asleep and left her there, and now they would face one another, just as soon as Virginia opened the door and went out.

It was going to be unpleasant she knew, but far less unpleasant than that horrible evening and night.

She went to the door, turned the handle confidently, then sighed. It didn't disturb her the door was still locked. She knew from the faint light it was barely dawn. Miss Tarks was asleep of course. She had left the door locked so her visitor wouldn't come running into the bedroom, crying and making a scene and waking her up. Virginia had a sudden picture of Miss Tarks in bed—all curlers and bleary eyes, with her face fallen in and her mouth screwed in in tight wrinkles. One of the Lady Helps had looked like that one morning when Virginia had peeked into her room. There'd been a glass on the bedside table too, with two rows of teeth grinning all by themselves through the glass.

She started to giggle, then sobered, going to the sink and carefully washing, drying herself slowly on one of the little fluffy hand towels Miss Tarks kept in the sink drawer. There was nothing she could do about her hair, except brush it back with her hands. That done she ate another biscuit, drank a little more milk—being careful to leave enough in the bottle for Miss Tarks' early morning tea—then went to the window.

The tree in the courtyard didn't sparkle in the faint grey light of dawn. The bit of harbour water she could see was grey, too. And the windows all round the court were blanketed by blinds—faceless, shutting her out.

Leaning on the sill she heard the low rumble of sound that always fascinated her. Lions. She loved the roar of lions for breakfast. It only happened sometimes. When the wind was blowing from the zoo, her father said. She wondered what they were roaring about this morning. Her father had said once he supposed they had a naughty daughter who'd woken them too early.

She laughed at that remembrance, laughed again at the idea of Miss Tarks in bed, being woken, and opening her toothless mouth like a lion and trying to roar.

She slipped down from the window, went over to the door and put her eye hopefully to the keyhole. Last night there'd been only darkness. This morning the dawn light was drifting into the room as it was into the kitchen. She could see only dimly, but she could make out a corner of a chair, a shoe...

It was Miss Tarks' shoe. She knew that quite well. And there was a foot in it. She could see it. And a little stretch of leg in pale nylon stocking. She couldn't see anything else, because the chair was in the way.

She huddled herself down on the breakfast bar bench, trying to think.

Miss Tarks wasn't going to roar like a lion. That was obvious. She wasn't in bed either. She was lying in there, in the other room, on the floor.

It was so absurd it wasn't even frightening. She went back to the keyhole and had another look, then she rattled the handle and called the woman's name.

Dead drunk. The phrase filtered absurdly into her

thoughts. Her father had said that once when a man in the street had tottered and fallen down. Her father had been furious and had picked her up, pressing her face into his shoulder as he'd carried her past the man, while he'd muttered about the man being dead drunk and a disgrace.

She couldn't possibly imagine Miss Tarks staggering and reeling and singing out and falling down. So she wasn't dead drunk. Which left what? Dead, she thought instantly, appallingly.

Terrified now, she remembered her mother had died all in a moment. Her Aunt, the one who lived now in Perth, had spoken of it once in Virginia's hearing, saying, "All in a flash. She was talking. Actually talking to us and she just clasped her throat, like this, and fell down. She never got up again. It was Heart they said. She'd had a bad heart for years and had never known."

She went back to the bench, huddling there, too scared now even for fears.

I have to get out of here, she thought, and ran back to the door, crying through the keyhole, beating on the door, turning away towards the wall and rejecting knocking on that because of what had happened in the night.

She ran to the window, slid it open as far as it would go, leaning out crying out, but none of the blinds moved, and her voice seemed an impossibly frail thing that the brisk breeze took and whisked away into the sky, leaving only the sound of some radio starting up in a flat below.

Going to the cupboard she fetched out the packet of biscuits again. Eating was something to do and it might stop her feeling sick, she thought. Perhaps if she concentrated on something else for a bit she might think better. She concentrated on the packet, spelling the letters, trying to read it properly.

The first word was too long. She ignored it and went on to the second. That was "We" and the next was "Help". "We help you feed your..."

She blinked, then laughed. How clever she was. All she had to do was put a notice in the window, saying Help!

That was it. Soon people would get up and they'd stretch and yawn and look out the windows at the day and the courtyard and the other windows and they'd see her notice and cry, "Look, there's a little girl who needs *Help*. Quick, run and help her . . ."

It took her ten minutes to realise there was absolutely nothing in the kitchen to make a notice. There were dishes and cloths and towels and saucepans, jugs and cutlery and dozens of other things, but no paper to write on, or a board or a slate or anything else. Only newspaper, and she couldn't see a word standing out plainly on a sheet of that.

Anyway there was nothing to write with. She found that out after another search.

It was still only grey dawn and the light wouldn't change for a while yet she knew, so she still had time to think of some way to make a sign.

It was the Christmas tape that gave her the idea. It was wide red sticky-backed tape, overprinted with holly, and there was a big roll of it in a drawer, with a pair of scissors. She wondered what Miss Tarks had wrapped up with it while she fetched it out and carefully cut it into sections, remembering the school break-ups when the class had made letters on cards from fancy tape just like this. The strips proved horribly hard to handle because they kept getting twisted and wrinkling up so she couldn't stick them properly to the glass, but after a long while, when the day was just starting to tinge the sky with pink, she had the letters, wobbly-looking, but quite clear in their outline, straggling across the glass.

. . .

Well here it was, Robbins thought, throwing open the door and going outside. Christmas Day, the day of days and by the time the sun went down he would bet anything half of them would be sick of it and disappointed into the bargain.

For himself, he hadn't expected anything different from

any other day, so it made no difference. There was satisfaction of sorts in that. He went round into the courtyard, surveying it with another tinge of satisfaction, because his expectations were justified.

There was a litter of empty cigarette packs and bent and twisted stubs, matches, screws of lolly papers, even ... he surveyed the little scatter with mild surprise ... even some broken dried up savouries. He wondered in faint amusement whose stomach had rebelled so he'd tossed his party quota of them out the window.

It was always the same—every morning the whole year round, though not as bad as this morning. Weekends were pretty bad, weekdays usually fairly good, but always someone in the court had found a bit of rubbish in their hands, and an open window at their elbows, and out the rubbish went.

Yet they hadn't known, most of them, that there was a caretaker. Who did they think swept away their bits and pieces?

Kicking at the broken savouries he decided that Christmas or not, holiday or not, he might as well sweep up. He was supposed to, anyway, though he wasn't fully on duty, but between supposed to do and doing he'd had the vague hope there'd be a vast gulf.

His gaze lifted, going up the stretch of windows. Just as he'd thought—the savouries had probably come out the Hickens' window. That had been some party all right. He'd sneaked up around midnight to the sixth floor to listen, and the noise, even on the landing, had been frightful.

Grinning, he wondered what time old Tarks had gone to sleep. Or maybe she hadn't. Maybe she'd hopped on her broomstick and flown away to quieter places. He wouldn't have put it beyond her.

He frowned, exclaimed in outrage, as he saw the windows. Didn't she know the rules? Of course she did, though. No decorative effects on windows. That was the rule. They were too hard to get off, and sometimes people didn't bother for weeks and weeks. You could see the result in some of the other buildings like this—weary, fading Santa Claus faces and greeting messages all over the glass. Horrible.

He squinted his eyes at the window, then pulled out his spectacles, breathing on the lenses and rubbing hard before slipping them on. He shook his head. Stopped half way perhaps, he wondered. Started to paste on a greeting and then ... but he couldn't see *her* wanting to decorate windows. Didn't make sense, but ... oh yes it did, he realised, seeing the small figure who was now leaning out from the sixth floor, waving. The kid, of course. She'd be messing around, but whatever she'd tried her hand at was just a mess of red squiggles so far as he could see.

He turned his back on her. He didn't feel like waving back. She was a holy terror and if he waved and old Tarks caught her leaning out...

Oh yes, *he'd* cop the blame. She'd be on the phone in two seconds spitting at him, telling him he was trying to break the kid's neck.

He walked away, rigid with indignation, promising himself he wouldn't come back to sweep up till the kid was at breakfast. Then no one could accuse him of making her act the fool.

. . .

Aldan's waking was a swift thing, too. Remembrance was equally swift, bringing panic. He went padding to the window, barefooted, peering out, while reaching impatiently for his spectacles and putting them into place.

He cried out with shock then. He was sweating in sheer panic when he realised it was all right, but the shock had been terrible.

It wasn't fair, he thought furiously. Shocking him like that. It simply wasn't fair. For a moment he'd thought those three windows were blazing with light, but they weren't. It was the sun on them, that was all. They were the only windows in that floor block that didn't have the blinds drawn still, and the sunlight had been fully on them, catching at the unshaded glass...

That was all it was. Wasn't it? His heart was still thudding and he went to his case, scrabbling among the things, coming up with the old fieldglasses that he'd had for years, and had packed in with his few meagre possessions for his trip.

Focusing them he looked across, and gave a jerk of laughter. Oh yes, he could afford to laugh at himself, couldn't he? The reflection was one of wry amusement.

Then he stared. Why hadn't he noticed that before? Why hadn't those marks... and what were they?... shown up last night? He refocused the glasses for a better view. The sunlight was a nuisance, because it blurred his vision of the glass. Without it, he thought in sudden fury, he might have been able to peer a little into the room beyond because the early morning air was so clear.

What the devil was it? Squiggles on the glass? That was crazy, but ... Christmas decorations, perhaps? He went on staring, wondering about it.

Not squiggles, he realised after a while. It was straggling, crooked letters. Letters back to front.

Help.

He went on staring, in amazement now, knowing that someone in that room beyond the glass must have put the straggling letters there, asking the world outside to come and help them. Someone too ... what, he wondered. Too weak, ill, injured? The word leaped out at him. Someone too badly hurt to remember the word they'd written made sense only to someone inside the room—that outside it was a jumble of nothing, unless you puzzled over it and finally made sense of it.

Isobel, he thought.

Not dead at all, but injured and calling for help.

He shook his head, refusing to believe it. It didn't add up. If she was alive, calling for help, there was the phone, there was her front door. She had only to open that or lift the phone and call the police. If she could have reached that window, she could have reached the phone, or the door.

He went on staring, numbed, holding onto the one thing that was fact, and not speculation, gazing blankly at that abortive cry for Help to the world beyond the glass.

CHAPTER ELEVEN

Why didn't they wake up, Virginia wondered. How *could* they lie in bed so late on Christmas morning, with all their presents to open and the day's fun to savour? Even the nice man who had trimmed his tree and waved to her was still in bed.

Virginia leaned out, gazing hopefully at each window, peering down at the court. Robbins was a stupid man, she thought dispassionately. A silly stupid man. Or maybe his eyes were funny. How else could she explain away him not seeing her notice and not answering her wave by waving back and running inside, and coming to let her out.

She had gone back several times to peer through the keyhole in the hope the foot would have moved and that Miss Tarks had had only a terribly long faint and was waking up, but each time the foot and the shoe had been quite still, and there'd be no answer—not even a mumble, a cry for help—from the other room.

After the last attempt to rouse the woman she simply forgot her. There seemed no logic in going on thinking about someone who couldn't help. She had boiled herself an egg, and cut some bread and butter, and had slathered . . . simply slathered . . . it with jam, because there was no one now to scold her or hit her or call her a greedy little pig.

She was washing her dishes when the phone rang. She had replaced the receiver when she had carefully straightened the room that morning and now she nearly dropped it in an eager snatch at it. She heard the voice, the words, through a blur. She cried, "Daddy, daddy . . ." and the voice was telling her to hold on, her daddy would be on the line in a moment, that this was a trunk call, and to wait just a few seconds.

Then her father was saying, "Ginny? Merry, merry Christmas, Ginny love, Ginny, I wanted . . ."

"Oh daddy," her voice rose shrilly, "come let me out! I'm locked up, daddy! She locked me up! Daddy..."

"Oh Ginny," his voice was over-riding hers, sorrowful, tired now, "you naughty girl! What've you been doing? You must have done something wicked, Ginny..."

She was so shocked that he hadn't said that of course he was coming immediately, right now—that she should run straight to the locked door and wait, that she blurted out, "I broke the glass bowl," and he was saying, "Ginny, you're terrible. She was doing such a Favour, Ginny and..."

"But I'm not. Daddy, daddy, come let me out! She's just lying..."

"Oh no," his voice was loud, drowning hers. "She wouldn't lie about you breaking it, Ginny. You're ... look, say you're sorry and the door will open, and then there'll be Christmas dinner. No, no Ginny," his voice drowned hers completely now, "I can't come. You've been naughty. I can't come. Goodbye. Be good. Say you're sorry. No, no, Ginny, I can't come. Goodbye."

She threw the receiver down, went running to the window, screaming, leaning out, seeking desperately for a face, an eye looking into her own.

Blank glass windows faced her. Noise swelled a little from radios tuning in as residents awoke. Her own cries dwindled and died. She stood staring into the empty court, at the Christmas tree, waiting till someone came, someone who'd see her wave and look up and see she needed help.

. . .

He had brought the glasses with him, slung by their strap over his shoulder. He'd slipped on sunglasses, was wearing a hat and had removed his lower plate so that his face looked entirely different to normal, and had darkened his skin with sun-tan lotion. He looked nothing at all like Frank Aldan, or Herbert Baring. He was again the man who had called on Isobel the previous evening.

The building seemed immense when he stood in the courtyard near the decorated tree, in its shadow, staring up, pinpointing the windows he wanted. There was no one about, except...

He stared. The small fluttering hand was barely visible against the sun-washed brick and glass. He moved closer against the tree, flicking the glasses out of their case, lifting them and focusing.

Her small face, anxious, the hair tumbled round it, seemed to leap down at him.

After a little he lowered the glasses again. His mind had gone completely blank. After another few seconds he told himself that after all it couldn't be Isobel's window. He'd made a mistake. There couldn't be a child there in Isobel's home. There simply couldn't be.

He focused the glasses again and went on staring while he remembered every action of that fifteen minutes of the previous day. He'd gone through the glass doors into the foyer, he reflected. There'd been no need to look for Isobel's name on the directory on the wall. He'd known the number and the floor.

The lift had been empty. He'd gone smoothly up. To the sixth floor. He'd turned right. He'd pressed the bell. He could clearly remember the look on Isobel's face as he'd forced her back into the hall with the thrust of his body. They'd spoken a little, he remembered and then what? He'd asked to see the place, that was it.

And ... he remembered now. Remembered the quick turn of her head. Towards the kitchen that had been and her startled eyes had made him wonder if she had a visitor.

That was why, he remembered now, he'd made straight for the room, to make quite certain they were alone in the place. But had he made absolutely sure? Of course not he realised grimly. He hadn't expected a child. A child could have darted out of sight, under a table ... could have been playing some game, meaning to jump out on Isobel and cry, "Booh!"

And then ... he was remembering again Isobel's expression when he'd come out again. She'd been ... yes, puzzled. He'd thought then it was puzzlement about his own appearance, but now ... he wasn't so sure. She'd followed on his heels while he'd toured through the other rooms, then had followed him back to the sitting room.

She'd headed straight for the kitchen then. He remembered that too, now. She'd gone in one second after they'd come back to the sitting room—darting in, in a hurry. He thought of that and of her excuse that she wanted to turn off the stove.

He could see her coming back, standing facing him with her back to the door, her hands behind her so he'd thought for a minute she'd brought out something to throw at him and he'd accused her of it. She'd jeered at him, bringing her hands into view, smoothing her apron, putting one hand into the pocket of it.

He knew now what she'd been doing. She'd been turning the key on the child, so it couldn't come out and meet him, or listen to their talk!

It was as plain as the nose on his face—now, that she stood there, turning the key, lifting it from the lock and slipping it into her apron pocket so he wouldn't wander back in there without her knowing.

He was gulping. Gulp after gulp that he couldn't stop. He was fighting down panic, the desire to run, and welling curses at his stupidity, and anger against the dead woman.

She had to be dead, he told himself. She was dead all right. And the child was locked in and unable to get help. She couldn't reach the front door, that was evident, or the phone ... that must be in another room or she'd have answered him the previous night, or rung for help.

She was doing the only thing she could think of, putting a cry for help on the window, only she hadn't realised it wouldn't show as Help the other side of the glass.

But soon someone was going to read it properly. He was sure of that. They'd see her fluttering hand, going on and on and sooner or later they'd read it...

And even if she couldn't describe Frank Aldan as he really looked, she must have heard his voice. He tried to remember how much he'd said, standing in the kitchen doorway, wondering too how much she might have heard through a locked door.

He remembered touching the door, thinking it was like a sheet of thin plywood. He could imagine the child with her head to it, listening, and he thought of all he and Isobel had said and knew he was in real trouble. The kid was going to spill everything they'd said. There'd be no If and Maybe and Perhaps about it if the police caught up with him now.

And there was Greta. How had everything managed to go so completely wrong for him? He stood there shaking with rage against a fate that had damned him completely. There was the child, condemning utterly. There was Greta, knowing where he'd gone, there was the time lag he'd hoped for. He wouldn't get that now either. It might be only a few hours before the kid was noticed and set free.

He'd counted so much on having time. That had been his last thought before sleep, that he still had time. Lots of it. Time to get to New Zealand, change his appearance completely, and vanish.

Now there wasn't going to be time even, and once the wretched brat talked...

He focused the glasses again, and the anxious, frightened little face leaped across space so that it seemed she could have touched him with her fluttering fingers.

A child, he reflected. Nothing but a child. Who was she? She hadn't been missed so far. It was a certainty that Isobel must have been minding her for Christmas. It didn't seem like Isobel to take on a child, but it must have happened.

How long before she was missed? If her small hand didn't flutter there, if her appeal for help was gone, how long would it be before she was missed?

She was nothing but a child. Nothing but a child . . . but a child who could talk . . . and condemn him utterly.

. . .

Was everyone in the world stupid, Virginia wondered in exasperation. She had waved and waved, but the person half hidden by the tree had gone without glancing up at her, and had gone casually, not hurrying as though he'd seen and was going to get help for her.

Perhaps he'd simply been interested in the tree, she reflected ruefully. He might have been gazing at that all the time and never even noticed her hand. That must be it of course. It wouldn't be long before someone came who *did* notice her and then it would be all right.

She tried to think of the wonderful moment when people realised and came running. They'd fuss over her and touch her and carry her away, offering icecream and toys, while crying to each other, "Think of it, just think of it. She was locked up like that and we never knew. Oh poor Virginia!"

Her small slumped body straightened as she saw Robbins. Even at that distance she knew it was Robbins. He was wearing his apron and had a broom. She watched him going slowly round the courtyard, sweeping. She waved to him, but he never once looked up.

She was furious with him. "Just wait till I get out of here," she told his bent head. "I'll ... I'll put papers and papers all round your horrid old court. I'll make you sweep and sweep and sweep till you cry. That's what I'll do. I'll drop papers and papers..."

Of course! She gave a jig of delight away from the window. She'd *make* him look up. She'd get out the newspapers from the cupboard and tear them into bits and drop them, plop, plop, plop, all over the courtyard, so he *had* to look up and see where they were coming from. Then he'd see her waving and see her notice and he'd come running.

The thought of how silly he'd feel and look when she told everyone how slow and stupid he'd been was balm to her spirits as she carried the papers to the window.

. . .

It was wonderful how the idea had come. One minute he had been in despair, the next the idea was there, fully planned, plotted out to completion.

He knew now it had been for the best and he had nothing more to worry about, not after he'd finished the job ahead. It was going to be written off as a frightful accident. He wouldn't have to worry about the police catching up with him and questioning him and perhaps arresting him.

It wouldn't be hard to get into the flat, he was sure. He hadn't examined the front door lock, but he could guess what it would be like. He knew enough about locks—had actually done a term of duty in the carpentry and locksmiths departments when he'd worked in the stores before meeting Isobel—to know how to force it without any tell-tale signs or damage afterwards.

He was going to open the lock and go in, closing the door gently behind him.

Then he'd knock. Softly. Very softly on that flimsy locked kitchen door. He'd speak to the child through it, telling her to be quiet and brave, that he'd have her out in a minute.

He'd get the key from Isobel's pocket where it must still be, and he'd insert it in the lock and turn it.

The child wouldn't have a chance to fight. He might shut her in one of the cupboards in the place while he dealt with Isobel, carrying her into the kitchen and placing her carefully on the floor

There wouldn't even be blood to worry about. He remembered how she'd fallen, spread-eagled on a white sheepskin mat in front of one of the chairs. Afterwards he'd be able to roll up the mat and take it away with him. The way Isobel lived, he doubted if anyone would ever know exactly what she had and didn't have in the place, so it wasn't likely a finger could point and say it was gone. If they did, what did it matter? You couldn't read anything into a missing rug.

He'd stretch Isobel out, carefully. Then he'd fetch the child and press her small hands round the gun and drop it, near Isobel's body.

No ... he amended that. First he'd deal with the door. He'd gently work and loosen at the handle. That first, then he'd deal with the gun and drop it. The child wouldn't fight. One swift blow to her neck, in the right spot and she'd drop down unconscious and never know a thing about any of it.

He'd take her to the window then, make sure no one was about and drop her out.

He'd go swiftly through the door then, slamming it. The loosened handle would simply fall off inside the kitchen. His departure would be unnoticed. Even if anyone heard her descent to the hard courtyard, attention would be on the court itself, not on the front entrance. He'd be gone long before any uproar started.

It was so simple really. When the police came to investigate things the whole story would be easy to read. The whole set-up would look like a child guest, prying where it had no right, coming on a frightened spinster's protection against trouble. The police, looking into the dead woman's background, would realise she might well get hold of a gun when her one-time attacker was due for release, and keep it by her for a time, forgetting till too late that it was loaded, ready for trouble.

So ... the child gets hold of it. It would be so easy from that point to picture an accident—the woman turning in horror and making a grab for the gun, and the child's hands tightening in defiance and fright. Then there would be a shot and Isobel would fall.

A frightened, terrified child would run for the door then, yanking at the handle, and if that happened to be loose it would simply come off in her hand and fall to the floor, so that the door stayed closed and she couldn't possibly get it open.

And then ... of course she'd try to get help. Her straggling, pathetic message on the window fitted in beautifully, he reflected. Even her waving fitted in. What more likely she would lean out, trying to attract attention, and overbalance and fall?

It fitted. Perfectly.

CHAPTER TWELVE

Rapidly, easily, she pulled the newspapers apart. She could see Robbins still going slowly along with his broom, his head bent. She let the first sheet of paper go and cried out in sharp annoyance because the breeze instantly caught it and lifted it, upwards, not downwards towards Robbins and the court. She watched it scudding away, to drop past the tree a little while later.

She balled the next sheet roughly before throwing it. It fell behind Robbins and well to one side, but she wasn't discouraged. She went on balling the sheets and throwing them till the courtyard below was littered and Robbins was up to the area where the sheets had fallen.

She saw him lift the broom, shaking his head. She threw two more balls, and he lifted his head, looking up.

She waved, tossing another ball of paper.

He stood staring, then lifted his broom. He shook it. He began to dance. He opened his mouth, mouthing at her, though the sound was carried away.

It was so absurd she started to giggle. He looked, she thought in shaking amusement, for all the world like one of the Christmas villains in the animated tableaux she had seen.

Tossing another ball of paper, she waved again to him.

Robbins shook his broom. He danced with rage. He mouthed and then he went, between walking and running, pausing at the corner of the building to shake his broom yet again.

She was breathless with laughter, then slowly sobered. Suddenly she realised he couldn't have seen her notice after all. But he was going to do something, she reassured herself. He was going to come up, she reflected in satisfaction. He'd ring and knock on the front door of the flat, and when there was no answer he'd get his master key and open the lock. He was so angry she was sure he wouldn't be defeated till he had his hands on her and made her stop throwing paper.

She sat back, folding her hands in her lap, waiting placidly till he came.

. . .

Leaderbee was glad it wasn't going to be a really hot day. The breeze was just right. The courtyard would be a lovely place with that. He'd decided he'd take his late breakfast as well as his lunch, to eat under the tree. He hoped some birds would come along. He'd brought some stale crusts for them if they did. He was excited at the whole idea and had dressed carefully in his best suit. It might be pretty shabby, but it was still his best, and he considered the day and the tree deserved it.

His steps slowed as he entered the courtyard. He was looking up at the windows, knowing he was hoping to see a small fluttering hand.

He was disappointed there was no sign of the child, but perhaps later on it would look out. He hoped so. He hoped it might even be allowed to come down, when it saw him picnicking there, and bring its Christmas toys and show him. That would put the seal of perfection on his day. It would make him feel as though he was looking at his own grandchild, and its toys—make him feel part of Christmas.

He settled his basket beside him on the bench, looking at the tree, at peace with the world, his faded eyes searching the windows for signs of life.

He saw the blind go up, saw a tousled dark head stuck out, and he smiled.

The young chap with the tree, he thought. The fellow had just rolled out of bed. Possibly he'd had a few long lonely drinks the previous evening and now had a bit of a head. But now he was awake and yes ... there he was, looking across the court at the child's window.

Leaderbee waved. For a moment he thought he wasn't

going to be seen, then the head came out a bit further, bending a little. A hand shot out, waving.

Leaderbee smiled. Nice young fellow, he thought. Perhaps later on, if he was going out to Christmas dinner, he'd stop in at the courtyard on his way and say Merry Christmas.

I'll offer him a bit of my cake if he does, he thought happily. The idea that the offer might lead to an offer from the young fellow, of a glass of something, was a warm feeling in his bones as he pulled his thermos from his basket, unwrapping the tiny parcel that was his breakfast.

. . .

Robbins was breathing gustily as he slammed inside, into his own flat, reaching for the phone. He found Miss Tarks' number after a pause that only made his temper worse. Then he dialled.

He wasn't going to mince his words. He wasn't going to so much as Christmas-mince them, he told himself bitterly, so that they came out a bit sweeter. He was going to give it to her and the kid hot and strong.

It was a surprise and shock when the child's voice abruptly cried out into his ear, at his barked, "Miss Tarks", "Come and let me out. Come and let me *out*!"

"Eh?" he jerked, then snapped, "You put Miss Tarks on the line you little imp. Go on, get..."

The voice shrilled, "Come and let me *out*! She locked me in and I can't get *out*. I can't make her hear and she's..."

Robbins gave a snort, between amusement and satisfaction. So that was it, he thought. Miss Tarks knew about the bowl and she'd locked the kid up and now the little wretch thought if she annoyed him enough he'd come up and make a stink so the old girl'd have to let her out...

"Oh no, my beauty," he broke in aloud. He said with gusty satisfaction, "I *know*! I know about that crystal and I know you broke it and pushed it down the chute! I got the pieces right here to show her. Oh yes, I know, miss!"

At the other end of the line Virginia was so startled she let out a little yelp. For a moment she forgot Miss Tarks wasn't answering anything, was maybe dead. She remembered only the bowl and the horrible agony of yesterday when she'd wondered when judgement was going to descend.

Then his voice was snapping at her, "You stay locked up and good riddance to you!" and she was speaking, crying, screaming into a silly dead thing that made no answering noise to all her entreaties.

. . .

Aldan came slowly to the glass doors to the foyer. He pushed them open and his feet whispered softly over the patterned green carpeting. The lift whispered, too. The place was quiet, as though half the great building was still asleep.

At the sixth floor it stopped gently and the doors slid, with a whisper of sound, to the left.

He went to step out, and stopped. After a moment the doors began to close. He let them. He didn't press the button again. He simply waited there in the lift's interior, looking pensively at the little artificial tree at the back of it.

It was maddening.

Who were they? he wondered.

Young people. A boy and girl.

Lovers perhaps, seeking a moment of privacy to talk.

But they couldn't stay there forever, with hands linked, in the passageway, in sight of Isobel's front door.

Sooner or later they'd move or be called inside one of the flats.

He cursed softly, pressed the sixth floor button again and when the doors slid gently aside once more, he looked out, hoping they might have gone, they were still there, oblivious of himself and the lift and everything but themselves. He wondered if they'd go if he stepped out, moving down the corridor.

It was worth a try. He put his handkerchief to his face, blowing heartily, walking briskly forward. They barely glanced at him as he went by. He went right down the corridor, then came back, but again they barely glanced at him before returning to their low-voiced talk.

He was furious, finding it appallingly difficult not to round on them, and rage at them and order them to get out of the place, telling them that it wasn't lover's lane.

He was shaking. He was shaking with the effort of keeping his control when he was in the lift again. He pressed the button, let himself sink down again to the ground floor, knowing he didn't dare hang round. He went out into the sunshine again, telling himself he'd give them twenty minutes, then try again.

. . .

When the hysterical pleading had died away she went back to the window, staring out. She saw the man by the tree, but was too tired to do more than stare. She was simply waiting—for all the blinds to go up, for people to stare out and see her message and do something about it.

She let her gaze flicker slowly over the windows she could see. A lot of the blinds had gone up already she noticed. She wondered why the people hadn't already come. It was a sort of ritual, window by window, which happened every morning. The blinds went up and someone—usually a man—leaned on the sill of the window, then yawned and stretched and stuck his head right out to peer up at the sky and gauge the weather. Then there was a long stare right round the court, and finally the head would go indoors and when you saw it next it was nearly unrecognisable, with the hair all slicked down, and teeth pushing cheeks out, and the dark stubble gone from jowls.

Usually she loved watching it. She couldn't make out why it hadn't apparently happened this morning. If it had people must have seen her message, she was certain.

There was a horrible little thought in one corner of her mind niggling at her, trying to force all other thoughts out, telling her that if her father and Robbins could misunderstand her, other people might, too. Other people in the building knew she was sometimes locked up. Perhaps they'd seen and thought...

She refused to let the thought take hold. Instead she thought of it being Christmas morning and she sighed in relief. *That* was why no one had come yet she decided. Christmas Day was different. There was no time or inclination for yawning and stretching and looking at the weather. You jumped out of bed and went skittering off to your pile of parcels. She could picture all the men and women in Nurrung Court, still in their dressing gown and pyjamas, opening presents and exclaiming in wonder and delight.

Later on, she thought hopefully, they'd get dressed and look out the windows, but then anxiety returned. She thought that perhaps they wouldn't look out at all. They'd hurry to dress and go to church and visit relatives.

Anxiously she leaned out, beginning to wave to the figure by the tree. He must have looked up at her window, and that excited her. He started to wave at once, and she couldn't make out why he wasn't taking any notice of her sign asking for help.

Then she thought, Maybe he's too old to see properly. Maybe he just sees my hand because it moved a bit. He knows it's a hand, waving. But he can't read what I've put on the window.

If she could only throw him a note, she reflected, it would solve everything. He wasn't like Robbins, she was sure. He wouldn't wave in such a friendly way if he was.

She remembered then that there wasn't any paper. Except newspaper. She could use that for a note, if she had something to write with.

She started to hunt through the cupboards again. Didn't Miss Tarks ever write notes at all she wondered. Everything was in such order it was easy to see at a glance that there was no pen or pencil anywhere. There was flour and oats and vanilla essence and what she called pink-icing colour.

She stared at it reflectively. It was red and would make a mark, she knew. She fetched a fork, but she couldn't get the red to stay on it—it simply slid off the silver surface and dripped away before she could write.

She sat on the floor, puzzling things out. She tried her finger, spilling a lot of the red colour on the floor tiles. She didn't care. Miss Tarks wasn't in a condition to do anything about it, that was obvious. But her finger proved to be no good. The colour seemed to sink into her skin and her finger was too big and made blobby marks, not letters at all.

She needed something like a pen nib she realised. A little thin thing. Her gaze roamed round the kitchen, settling on one thing after another, discarding them. She came to the stove and saw the matches and from then on it was easy. The letters weren't very neat or very well formed, but in the end she had a piece of newspaper with the white margin carrying a red appeal to let her out of the kitchen.

Carefully she labelled the sheet and went back to the window. The man was still there. She waited till she had his attention again.

Then carefully she let her waving hand hold it high, hoping he could make out what she was doing. Then she dropped the paper.

. . .

He'd make them pay, Robbins reflected bitterly, going back to the broom, slamming it back into its cupboard. He wasn't going to be made a fool of by a chit of a child and a wretched cranky woman.

Tomorrow, when the kid wasn't locked up and his own temper wasn't in such a boil, he was going up. That was flat. Old Tarks would still be cranky enough about her blasted bowl to loathe the kid like poison. Even though she loathed him too, she'd have to say thanks for the bowl and his telling her she might get it fixed someway or other. And then he was going to tell her that little imp could just come down and pick up every scrap of paper in the courtyard.

She'd be sour enough at the kid to let her do it, and pleased enough at getting the bowl back without having to pay to search for it, to stop any argument.

Oh, you'll pay right enough, miss, he thought grimly. You'll pay. The sauce of it throwing paper at me like that!

He wondered if she was still at it. Grimly he went outside again and round to the courtyard. It looked terrible. The wind had blown the paper balls all over the place and was busy unravelling them now. In the morning it would look ten times worse and the residents would start complaining.

Then his eyes narrowed. His choloric temper came to the full boil and boiled right over. It was the last straw! Now some crazy old tramp was in the court spreading more paper. He watched the greaseproof piece roll across the paving. It wasn't only paper, he saw in continued growing rage. It was bread crusts, too—great pieces of bread that the blasted birds would peck at and leave around for days.

He yelled, "You!" and the birds scattered and the old man looked up, staring. "What the hades're you doing in here? You're not a resident!"

He was up to the older man now. His gaze flickered knowledgeably, contemptuously, over the shabby neatness. "Who told you you could picnic here?"

Rodney Leaderbee was confused and shaken and ashamed. He had seen the knowledgeable glance over himself for what it was—an assessment of his position and poverty. For a moment he couldn't speak, then he answered shakily, "I've been here before. You've never said..."

"Not having a picnic, you haven't. Having a picnic and spreading crusts and paper in *my* court," he added bitterly, waving his hand round the cement area. "Look at it. You take your picnic elsewhere before I toss you out. Go on—beat it!"

Leaderbee's hands were shaking violently. They failed him when he tried to get everything back into the basket again. Another piece of paper escaped and helplessly he watched it go, seeing it mingling with all the other papers strewn there.

CHAPTER THIRTEEN

Megan woke with thoughts of the tree. She had dreamed of it. In the dream she had stood on a ladder fastening spun glass balls to the branches. She had been holding one as blue as the sky over summer paddocks, and suddenly two strong brown hands had fastened over hers and over the ball and she had turned to see the man from Nurrung Court.

She wished she hadn't dreamed at all because the waking to the small lonely room seemed all the worse.

For a little she lay there, watching dawnlight fill the window and spread fingers of light into the room. She waited till the light actually touched the pillow and then she sat up. It was her for the bathroom, she knew; the hour when the old couple would keep religiously to their own quarters, so they wouldn't be accused of invading her privacy.

But this was Christmas morning and her cheeks were flushed, her eyes brightening. When she went out into the little hall this morning they'd be there she was sure. Both of them. Smiling and wishing her a wonderful day and asking her to share their Christmas duckling and home-made pudding.

She threw on a robe, grabbed her towel and wash bag, threw open the door and stopped.

The shiny linoleum winked at her derisively. The whole hall stretched emptily. At the end the bathroom door gaped wide. In an hour it would be locked again till her evening hour. Just in case she dared to intrude for one moment on their privacy.

It was laughable, yet she couldn't laugh. Meekly, submissive to the beckoning doorway, she went down, showered and came back. She dressed and waited, close beside her door that she left just a little ajar, so she'd hear them when they came to lock up the bathroom again.

She wasn't going to be left alone, ignored. She was determined on it, but when the old lady finally shuffled from the back of the house, swinging the key in her hand as she came, Megan's dart out was so violent, her Merry Christmas so loud, so aggressive, the old woman looked startled and shocked and bewildered.

"Dear life," her tone was disgruntled, "You half frightened the wits out of me."

"I'm sorry. I didn't want to miss you," Megan was whispering now, her spirits flagging, her aggression gone. She wanted only to slink away from the suspicious startled gaze. "I just wanted to wish you a Merry Christmas."

"Thank you," the white head nodded graciously. "The same to you I'm sure, Miss Tremont." She turned, the key slid into the lock and twisted and was pulled out. The old lady nodded again and shuffled away. A door banged, then the house was silent again.

Megan was left there, on the shiny, sun-touched lineoleum, knowing she was crying.

This is ridiculous, she thought fiercely. Utterly ridiculous! How can people go on like this! It's Christmas Day—a time for friendliness surely. But perhaps it was her own fault, she thought wearily, going back to her room and shutting the door. She'd frightened the old lady with that absurd darting out and loud, aggressive greeting. How were the old couple to know their tenant was alone anyway? They never pried or asked questions. She thought in wry amusement that probably they might be envying her youth this Christmas Day, sure that she'd be going out with friends to spend a boisterous, wonderful, exciting day.

Well, she wasn't going to stay home. She was determined about that. She'd have a picnic she decided. She'd leave her tiny pudding till evening, and take cake, some of the cold chicken she'd bought from the corner delicatessen, some fruit, and a thermos of tea, and go ... where? One of the beaches? She didn't really fancy the idea. Transport was sure to be crowded. It would be hot and exhausting and all the exhilaration of her outing would drain out of her. A park then? She thought of the nature strip by the harbour wall. Then thought of the tree.

Thinking of the previous evening, she remembered the old man saying that none of the residents ever bothered to come and stare and admire. There'd be no one then to object if she had a picnic by the tree. She could share her dinner with the birds and perhaps ... excitement touched her with fleeting fingers ... perhaps a hand would flutter from a window. Perhaps two would wave. Maybe the child would even come down to show her toys. She remembered her own childish excitement on Christmas Day—half the pleasure of having gifts was showing them off to everyone who came near.

Perhaps ... she shut her mind on the thought. No point in giving time to thinking of the possibility the man might lean out and wave too, and see her down there alone and come down, a filled glass in his hand, to drink a Christmas toast with her, to say Merry Christmas, to talk and touch her hand.

She piled everything, picnic, two magazines, some cake and bread for the birds, into a straw basket, then hesitated, thinking again of the child. She'd take something, she decided finally. If the child came down she could give her a tiny gift of some sort.

She settled at last on the tiny pottery squirrel. He'd cost only a few shillings at a second hand stall at Paddy's Market. She'd been simply killing time that morning she had wandered through the crowds, and had had the little creature almost forced into her bag by a brassy-haired woman with voice to match. She'd been faintly annoyed at the time, but the little thing was attractive and she had grown fond of it.

Not fond enough though to stop her giving it away, and it was the only thing she had that might appeal to a child. She wrapped it carefully in a twist of tissue paper, robbed her sewing box of a length of wide red ribbon to tie it and popped it into the straw basket with the picnic.

She was humming as she left the house, walking briskly

towards Nurrung Court, swinging the basket, at peace with the world for the moment, excited at the thought of what the day might bring her.

Both peace and excitement went as she stopped, staring. It was so appalling it might have been some television drama, she thought in sick distaste. There was the old man, shaking hands fighting with papers, a basket, a thermos, and a wedge of iced cake, while the younger man, face twisted into a scowl, hands on heavy hips, watched, jeering, "Don't mind me, old-timer, just let your papers blow all over the place. Go on. Why don't you? I'm only the bloke who'll have to clean up after you, you dirty old b . ."

He saw her then. His mouth fell open and he took a step back, his gaze appraising her, narrowing, then growing aggressive again. As he realised she had no right there either, she thought bitterly. She watched the expression change again, to anger, as his gaze flickered to her own basket, with the top of the thermos showing.

His mouth opened, then closed without sound as she looked at him, going forward.

She spoke not to him, but to the old man. The same one who'd been there the previous night, she realised, remembering the six daughters. She had laughed at the remembrance going home. She didn't laugh at it now.

She put her basket on the ground, bent, gathered things, and began to try to help the old shaking hands with the other basket as she said, "I'm sorry I was late. Did you drop your basket, grandpa?" Her gaze flickered up to the silent watching man. She felt the old hands beside her own become still. She said again, "We'll go on now to the park, grandpa. Come along."

She linked her arm in his and began to lead him away, not looking back, forgetting even the child, even the man with the baby Christmas tree.

. . .

Virginia saw Robbins come back and speak to the man by the tree. She was furious, because now the man might forget about the paper she'd thrown. She was quite sure he had seen it fall. He had started up, and a piece of paper had been blown away from his lap. He had been staring towards her paper when Robbins had come round the side of the building.

She saw them talking and the woman come. All three seemed to be talking and then...

Oh, it couldn't be happening! She leaned out, waving and crying to them, but no one paid her any attention. The man and woman were simply walking away and Robbins was following after them, while her piece of paper was gently bowling over the courtyard, to mix and mingle with all the rest of the paper she had thrown before.

. . .

When the lift doors whispered open Aldan stepped out, onto the carpeted corridor. The boy and girl were gone and the place was deserted. He heard the whisper of sound as the lift doors closed gently behind him again and he stepped forward.

He walked to Isobel's door, let his gaze flicker to right and left, stood still, listening. He could dimly hear a radio somewhere—a sound that was merely that—sound, without sense.

He bent slightly, inspecting the keyhole, the lock, straightening again smiling slightly. What fools people were, he reflected complacently. You put a lock on a door and handed the owner a key and they thought they were safe from anything, yet on this type anyone with a bit of knowledge could slide a sliver of card between jamb and lock tongue and force it back. It took patience of course. Patience, steady hands, and sometimes a bit of time.

His gaze flickered left and right again while his hand dipped into his pocket and came out. Without bending this time, standing straight as though waiting for someone inside to open the door, he put out his hand, gently moving it, allowing the lip of the card to angle in between jamb and tongue.

Then he was still. He didn't make a sharp movement

when he let the card disappear back into the palm of his hand, and the hand drop to his side. He did it leisurely. He didn't turn either, though his fear was screaming out at him to do so, to see what the sound further along the corridor had been; to see what was happening away to his right.

He still didn't move even when he realised someone was coming towards him. He kept his face turned towards the door, gazing at it, while his left hand reached for the bell. A woman's voice said in his ear, "Don't ring for a tick."

He didn't want to turn and face her, but it would have looked too strange if he had gone on ignoring her. He told himself that it didn't matter anyway, if she saw him and remembered him. He didn't look like Frank Aldan. or Herbert Baring. And Isobel's death wasn't going to be called murder. It was going to be written off as a terrible double accident.

He had turned, asking, "Why not?"

She looked tired and was huddling a pink chenille wrap round herself. She looked more like a bolster than a woman he thought, with the wrap and her hair tied up in a fluffy pink scarf.

She said breathlessly, "Because I'm not dressed for her to see me. But look—you're a friend, eh?" She didn't wait for an answer, but rubbed a hand over her forehead and said, "I heard the lift. The damn thing makes a funny sort of whine in our bedroom when it goes up and down. Don't ask me why. It doesn't seem to make a sound when you're in it, but in our room ... but what the hell! You're not interested. But I was ... stickybeaking ... seeing who it was who'd come up here. And I saw you here, and ... look, tell her we're sorry, will you?"

"But you don't know, do you? Lord, I'm tired." She stifled a yawn. "We're next door. Hickens is the name. We threw a party last night. She nearly had a fit. Rog was in a temper or else we wouldn't have done what we did." She yawned again, "Lord, I'm in a muddle. Listen—I'll tell you what happened. Understand?" she asked at last.

At his nod she went on heavily, "We were both ashamed after. The party was a hell of a lot too noisy and that's a fact. It got out of hand that . . . well, we've got to live here. So has she. And we shouldn't be going on like this. Like a bunch of kids spiting one another, so I said to Rog. And look—it's *Christmas,*" she gazed at him pleadingly. "This is the time for burying old scores, isn't it? So look, tell her from us we're sorry. Both of us. Tell her we'd like her to come round this evening, to supper. We'd like to apologise, and try to make friends and start off the new year decently. Will you do that?"—

"Yes."

Good god, he wondered angrily, wouldn't the wretched woman ever go? She was going on babbling about Christmas, and new year resolutions and being sorry, while he simply stood there sweating, with the minutes flicking by and heaven knew what was happening at the back of the flat where the child was leaning out the window.

He breathed a sigh of relief when a whisper of sound heralded the lift coming up again. The woman jerked, said, "My God!" and fled back to the open door further along, throwing over her shoulder, "Don't forget. And thanks," before the door banged shut.

His gaze flicked past the closed door, to the lift. He almost swore aloud, staring in white rage at the two women. Two women armed with a vacuum cleaner and a big bag on wheels, and mops.

Cleaners—on Christmas Day! It was impossible.

He turned from the door, went rapidly towards them. They grinned, calling, "Merry Christmas, sir."

He stopped, turning half from them, asking in a voice that was hardly a whisper because more sound would have taken away the last of his control and made him rage at them. "Surely you're not working today of all days."

One of them laughed, shook her mop blithely, said, "This is one day when cleaning up is needed. Lots of parties Christmas Eve and lots of visitors over the hols. There'd be complaints to the managing agents if there was a mess for them to see, wouldn't there now? Look at that now..." she pointed.

He saw the scatter of used matches, cigarette stubs and paper that spattered the carpet.

He said loudly, "Disgraceful," and went past them, pressing the lift button.

. . .

Leigh Warner woke late and lay back smoking for a while. There was nothing to get up for. A parcel had come the previous day from his sister down south. He hadn't opened it. Wasn't interested in it even now. There would be a shirt in it, he knew, his exact size and white and drip dry. The perfect shirt for a lonely bachelor. There'd be a small cake, too. There'd be a box of cigarettes from his brother-in-law and a crayonned Christmas card from his nephew.

None of it meant much, not when you were six hundred miles from the givers and were alone. He couldn't so much as ring them and hear their voices, because they were spending the holiday camping.

Reluctantly he pulled himself upright and faced the day. Remembering the child, the one touch of companionship in his Christmas, he went to the window, leaning out, but she wasn't there. He grinned suddenly. He'd received one of the little circulars from the managing agents telling him not to decorate his windows, or else. It had mildly annoyed him. But rules didn't mean anything to children. He wondered what she had been trying to put on the glass—it looked like nothing on earth.

His gaze flickered down. He saw the waving hand near the Christmas tree and remembered the night and the lights and the two figures below and the game they and the child and himself had played.

Vigorously he waved back. Who was it down there, he wondered as he showered. Another resident? Another one alone? He doubted it. It was probably some husband of one of the retired couples, pushed outdoors while his wife got on with cooking their turkey and pudding.

Later he went back. The child was there again. He could see her more plainly in daylight, but he eyed her frowningly, disapprovingly now, because she was leaning too far over the sill.

His gaze followed her own. He saw Robbins and recognised him even at that distance, from the apron. Then his gaze focused on sunlight shining on a cap of fair hair and he was remembering the previous evening, the girl's caplike hair and her mocking greeting. He told himself it couldn't be the same girl, even while he remembered the way she had looked at him sharply when he'd mentioned living at the court. He'd thought then she'd been about to say something, but her lips had tightened and she'd remained silent in the end.

He wondered if it was really the same girl, if she lived here, had wanted to tell him so, had wanted to say she was alone. Like himself. She might, like himself, be in some borrowed flat. But who was the man?

They seemed to be arguing with Robbins, too.

He watched them starting to move away. He leaned further out, willing them to look back, but all three of them disappeared round the corner of the building. He realised that the child was waving to him alone now. Waving and calling, the wind catching her voice, distorting it so he couldn't make out what she said.

He knew what it was though. He leaned out, waving, calling back to her gaily, "Merry Christmas, Merry Christmas, have a happy day," and hoping she could hear.

Then he forgot her. He was simply thinking of the girl.

He was going down, he knew. He was going to run down and meet up with them in pretended casualness and see if it was the girl of the night before. If it was . . . he could ask her, couldn't he, if she lived in the place?

He went out, banging the front door behind him, pressing the lift button, furious that the lift didn't come immediately.

. . .

HG—H

Virginia found it impossible to believe the nice man could be so stupid. He wasn't old, she told herself pettishly. He didn't have bad eyes, surely. He must have seen her notice. He *must* have.

And she'd cried out to him, and he'd only laughed.

Laughed at her. Oh, that didn't make sense at all, she thought in bewilderment. How could anyone laugh and mouth things back. She hadn't been able to hear what he'd said, but she'd seen his smile.

Oh, it didn't make sense. Not ... unless he thought like Robbins, that she was naughty and locked in for misbehaviour. That horrible thought was back—the fear everyone was going to mistake her plea on the window.

She stared helplessly at the empty window across the court. She could see the little tree, but the man had vanished. Then hopefully she saw another window, further down, slide open. A woman's head peered out.

Virginia screamed. She waved, leaning out, screaming out to the head.

It lifted. A hand came up and waved.

Appallingly, the white face smiled. It mouthed. The head bobbed, the hand waved, the mouth opened and closed and the lips smiled. The head turned, and looked back into the room behind, and another head joined it. An old man's. It leaned out, the sun shining on its baldness. The mouth smiled. The head bobbed, the lips mouthed, and another hand waved to her.

. . .

The woman laughed. She said, "Doesn't it take you back, Roy, to the kids on Christmas day? Oh dear, I miss them so! Don't you remember Tess leaning out like that, calling and waving to passers-by at Christmas. Takes you back doesn't it? Vera and Tess always used to play that way. Go on wave to her again, Roy. What a lovely game she's having."

CHAPTER FOURTEEN

Aldan had gone back to the tree. He stood there, appalled, watching the child's hand fluttering and the other hands, from the second floor, right at the corner, almost above his head, fluttering in answer. He could hear cries. From the child, he knew.

He expected an uproar, then saw the smiles on the faces above his head. Smiles, he thought and panic went. It was all right after all he realised. They thought it was all a game.

For the time being he was safe, but she wasn't going to be safe for ever. Sooner or later someone closer to her was going to open a window and lean out and hear what she was crying, see her face closely enough to know there was trouble, see the window and puzzle over it and realise the truth.

After a few minutes the couple on the second floor gave a final wave, stepped back and the lace curtains fell into place over the open window.

He focused the glasses, staring upwards. The child's face seemed to leap down towards him again. She didn't look frightened and absurdly he was glad of that. He was glad she was feeling angry. Her small face was contorted in rage.

His hands slipped on the glasses and dropped them as the voice said, "What're you up to? Here, let's have a gander," and a hand caught at the falling glasses, fielding them neatly.

He swung round, violent emotion flaring and dying at the same time. It was too late to stop the other man, too late to strike at him. Aldan began to turn, knowing only a frantic desire to get away, to escape and hide.

He stopped.

The man was laughing and that seemed incredible.

Aldan stopped in mid-step, slowing and turning and realised that not only was it possible, it was really happening. The other man was laughing.

He was saying, his words savouring enjoyment, "Ah, look at her. In a terrible temper you are, miss, but a fat lot of good it'll do you. Oh, it won't help you, my lady. Look at her, screwing up her face and banging her fists on the window." He let the glasses fall, still gazing upwards. He said sourly, "If she breaks *that* glass there'll be hell to pay."

Then he swung round, glaring at his companion. "You aren't a resident, mate. What're you staring here for?"

Silently Aldan held out his hand, averting his face, pretending to stare upwards. "My glasses, please. No, I'm not a resident," he said at last, half whispering. "I'm staying round here. I saw your tree, then the child. She . . . was leaning out . . . that's dangerous . . ."

He couldn't make head nor tail of the man's obvious enjoyment over the child's rage and plight. He *had* to know what was going on in the other's head. He went on whispering, catching at the glasses, holding them tightly so the other man shouldn't get them back again, "Why is she in such a temper?"

"She's locked up, see. She's a holy terror. You've no need to worry she'll fall and break her neck. Only the good die young. *That* one'll see out her hundredth birthday. She's staying there for Christmas and she busted up some crystal. Now she's locked up. She's *always* getting locked up, or locked out of her home altogether, see."

He turned on his heel, and started to move away. He didn't look back, or even say goodbye.

Aldan went on standing there. How incredible life was, he was reflecting. You thought you were done for and all the time things were falling into place for you, making you safe. The man was the caretaker. He couldn't be anyone else. Now if someone saw that notice, heard her cry out, rang down to him to find out what was happening, there'd be nothing done.

Nothing at all. Until too late.

. . .

Leaderbee was conscious of only one thing—that the girl had saved him from complete humiliation. She had stopped that man from ranting and railing at him; had turned him, with a few words, from a piece of human debris into someone who was called Grandpa. He had seen, in that moment, the change in the other man's eyes. The contempt, the desire to hurt, had been replaced by something else—a wary acknowledgement that his victim had a champion to stand up for him.

He was grateful to her, but he felt quite ill. It was partly shock, partly disgust and humiliation, partly fear. In a few minutes she was going to start asking about those mythical daughters of his, then the truth would be out and she would be deciding he shouldn't be alone and getting in touch with people ... and that meant the authorities.

He said violently, "I'm not going into a home!"

She stopped, half turning, still holding his arm, staring at him. "Did he say you should be in a home?" her voice was low, but angry.

Angry for him, he realised. He blinked. He said, "No. It was that young fellow in the out-patients. The doc, you know. As good as told me I couldn't look after myself because of my feet. I can't bend enough to dry them, see." He blinked again, sighed, gently took his arm from hers. "Thank you for helping me, miss. I can manage now. I got a bit sort of shaky when he roused on me that way. I was sitting there ... feeding the birds ... I didn't realise I was making a mess. I suppose ... he was quite right."

"He was horrible," she said still in that same low, angry voice. "Quite horrible. But I'm beginning to find out that a lot of people are horrible. Oh, sometimes they don't mean to be, but ..." she stopped. She said, "You were going to have a picnic, weren't you? Well so was I. Under the tree, too. And ... I thought that child might come down. I ... brought a present."

He was amazed, disgusted with himself that he hadn't had the same idea.

He didn't know what to say, and then suddenly there were

three of them walking together. A young man was there, pushing his glasses up his big bony nose and saying, "You're the girl in the newsagents who sold me the spun glass balls."

Leaderbee peered from one to the other of them and saw the girl was almost scowling. She said fiercely, "What's wrong with them? They were perfectly good balls..."

Leaderbee saw the young man blink. He thought for a minute they were all going to get at cross-purposes and there was going to be another row, then the young man said, "They were beautiful. You know that quite well. Why did you think I wanted to complain?" When she didn't answer, he went on, "You live here? In the court I mean? It was you, wasn't it, waving last night? To the child? To me? It was me up there. Did you know that?"

Megan admitted, "I thought it might be. You said Nurrung Court—there in the store. And there was the tree. A baby tree. And you were decorating it, so ... so ..." her eyes had turned to the old man.

"Leaderbee, miss."

If anyone had asked him what happened next he wouldn't have been able to say. It was all confused. He finally found himself on a seat by the harbour wall, with the young pair either side of him, and they were talking about the child, and the girl was holding up the tissue wrapped parcel with its perky red bow and telling them about Paddy's Market and the squirrel.

Leigh said, "I was going to ring her and wish her Merry Christmas, but I don't know them. The child, or the woman she's staying with. I don't know them at all."

Megan said in exasperation, "How mad that is! Just because you don't know someone's name you feel you can't even say Merry Christmas. Don't you see how crazy that is?"

"People misunderstand," Leigh began.

"Oh they do, but they shouldn't, and someone has to break the ice." She looked at the parcel in her hand. "I still want her to have it. She seemed such a friendly little thing—so ... so happy—playing like that ..."

Leigh stood up. He said, "Let's all go then. You to give her the squirrel, Mr. Leaderbee to say Merry Christmas, and me to take a bottle of sweet sherry for the old lady. Old ladies like sweet sherry don't they? Even if she doesn't . . ."

"She won't mind." Megan stood up. They each linked an arm through Leaderbee's.

His only thought was he should put a few things straight. He said shakily, "You know, miss, I haven't got six darters. Not really."

Leigh gave a shout of laughter. He grinned, his big nose looking bigger than ever. He said, still laughing, "Who wants six daughters? According to Robbins—that's your caretaker friend—one female child is more than a handful. He loathes our little hand-waver."

He felt sudden anxiety. He remembered the broken crystal bowl in the basement and Robbins' almost gloating dwelling on what would happen when Miss Tarks found out. He wondered if the finding out had happened already, if they'd be met at the door of the flat by a sour-visaged woman who denied them entrance, denied their Christmas gesture with a sourly voiced statement that the child had been too naughty for visitors or treats.

. . .

Deliberately, with something approaching glee, Virginia got out the small cake with its glossy untouched icing. She hadn't dared before to touch it, not even with Miss Tarks' foot lying so still the other side the door. She had dwelt on the possibility of the future with Miss Tarks well and striding about again and going to the cupboard and crying in awful tones, "Who's been at my cake?"

She still couldn't decide whether Miss Tarks was dead or not. It didn't help at all to think about that. She simply fetched out the cake and gained a wonderful satisfaction from cutting through the glossy white icing, into the satisfying richness beneath and then sitting there, in the now disordered kitchen, munching at it, her eyes half closed while she tried to think of something else to do—something to get herself out of the kitchen.

She was horribly sick of that kitchen. She was horribly sick of people too, she decided pettishly. They were stupid. Couldn't they realise that on Christmas Day of all days you were unlikely to be so horribly naughty you fetched a lockup as punishment? And couldn't they tell the difference between something that was a game and something that wasn't?

The cake finished, she simply wiped her grubby sticky hands down her pinafore front and went back to the locked door. The foot was there still in the same place. She sighed, rattled the knob again hopefully, then stopped.

How did you open sealed-up things, she pondered?

The answer came in a flash. You used a tin opener of course.

If a tin opener could open a tin she didn't see why it couldn't someway open a door.

She went and fetched it, eyed the steel point and the thin corkscrew attachment with pensive eyes, then jabbed the point into the keyhole.

It wouldn't go in very far, and all her rattling and twisting and turning did nothing at all to open the lock.

. . .

There was no answer at all to their ringing. They rang twice, and there was still no answer. They turned to gaze at one another a little foolishly—the fair haired girl with the tissue wrapped parcel; the big nosed young man with the carefully wrapped bottle, and the old man empty-handed but smiling bravely in the face of disappointment.

Megan said at last, "But the child's in there! They're not out. The child's in there, because she was waving to you two. You said so."

Leigh said in disappointment, "They might have gone out since. We wasted a lot of time. Or Miss Tarks might simply not want visitors today."

"That's ridiculous," Megan told him stormily and put her finger to the bell again.

The door remained closed, but abruptly Megan bent her

head, putting it close to the door. She said sharply, "I'm sure there's someone in there. I can hear a noise. Bumping. Something like that. In there. I'm sure it's in there, Leigh."

. . .

Virginia had such a shock when the bell rang that she dropped the tin opener. She stared upwards. There was a tiny red bulb on the wall. It had turned red and was relaying the sound from the door. For a minute she was so surprised at the idea of someone ringing the door bell that she simply went on staring.

Then she began to beat on the locked door. Her small bunched fists beat a rapid tattoo. She called, went on banging, thinking, It's them. It's the people below who waved and laughed at me. They've come after all.

But remembering the laughter and the mouthing faces, she shook her head. It was someone else, she decided. Someone else who'd looked out and seen her notice.

She had to stop beating because her hands were sore, and she didn't think they could hear her in any case. She thought happily that when no one came to answer their ringing they'd go down to Robbins and ask him to bring his key along...

She was suddenly panic-stricken again, remembering Robbins ringing on the phone.

"Oh, *he* won't do anything," she cried to the disordered kitchen. "He'll laugh and tell them I'm bad. I'm locked up, he'll say, because I was wicked. He'll tell them ... about the crystal bowl I put down the chute..."

Slowly she got up. She went over to the wall, ignoring the ringing now because she was sure whoever was out there wasn't going to help. She opened the chute and peered down. There was only blackness. She didn't think yelling down it would do a scrap of good. Her father had told her it went down and down and down—right down to the basement where it fell into a big box and later on Robbins burned the box in a big fire.

The same fire that helped heat their water. She remembered how fascinated she had been at that fact.

She remembered something else too—asking why she didn't feel the fire when she opened the chute. Her father had explained carefully that the rubbish didn't go straight to the fire. It went to the big box so Robbins could sort out the things that wouldn't burn easily and put them aside for the rubbish collection.

He'd said something else, too—about Robbins making a pretty penny out of things sent down by mistake. Why once, she remembered in rising excitement, her father had put down a paper—an important letter in an envelope. He had gone down and given Robbins some money and the letter had been found and given back to him. He had told her then that Robbins went through the rubbish just in case something like that happened with other residents.

So if she sent down a message some time soon Robbins would see it, she thought excitedly.

The only trouble was, Robbins wouldn't believe it. She was sure of that and slowly her excitement died away.

. . .

The three of them went back to Leigh's flat. He had said, "Well, they're out and that's that. You must be wrong about a noise, Megan—I can't hear a thing anyway. They're out. Come on to my place. We'll have a Christmas dinner of sorts down there. I didn't lay in much," he said ruefully, then saw their eyes. Withdrawn eyes. Eyes that asked, "Why should you imagine we can have Christmas dinner with you? Why imagine we haven't a lot of invitations to fulfil elsewhere?"

He was suddenly completely fed up—with conventions, with human pride, with hiding the fact of his own loneliness.

He said cruelly, "Or will you go back to your six darters, Mr. Leaderbee? And will you, Megan, go back to your family mansion, wherever that is and order the footman to bring in the pudding for a family of eighty!"

He thought for a minute she was going to walk away. Then the old man said, "You know I haven't got six darters. That was all nonsense. A bit of a fairy tale, like. Sounds silly I know, but ... I was lonely, you see. I was going to picnic out there. Cold stuff, like. I can't cook, that's the trouble. It's my hands ..."

Now he had started he couldn't stop. All the ridiculous, petty frustrations of his life—not being able to manage saucepans or drying his feet or lifting boiled clothes from the copper—came tumbling out along with his loneliness.

He was ashamed, humiliated, when he'd finished, but the girl glossed over it. She said, taking his hand in her own slim, warm, steady one, "It's the same with me, Mr. Leaderbee. Oh, I can cook all right and even dry my toes," she laughed a little, "though sometimes, after a day in the shop, I wish I didn't have toes at all, they hurt so much. But ..." she looked levelly at Leigh, "I haven't a mansion, or a footman, or a family. Not anyone."

Leigh said simply, "Come down to my flat. Both of you."

He and Megan each took one of the old man's arms again. They led him to the lift. The doors whispered open as they reached it. A man stepped out, not even looking at them because he was blowing his nose. He was walking down the corridor as the doors whispered shut, taking the three of them down to the fourth floor.

. . .

Virginia had closed the chute panel again. She knelt, trying to peer under the door, trying to get her fingers to wriggle under it, but the frame was so securely fitted there was no room at all.

She sat back on her heels. It was useless to think after all that perhaps the key had fallen out onto the floor on the other side, with all her rattling and banging, and that she might have been able to get her fingers round it.

The little red globe wasn't glowing now, or giving its shrill warning of a visitor, which meant the people outside had gone away. She didn't expect that they'd do anything. Not with Robbins to block them.

She picked up the tin opener, surveying it thoughtfully. The narrow corkscrew fascinated her. She knew you wriggled it into corks and twisted so the corks popped out. And you turned a key, wriggling it really, to open a door. She thought it might be possible that if she put the screw into the keyhole and turned it and wriggled it the door might pop open.

Encouraged by the idea she poked the screw in. It was a tight fit and it simply refused to wriggle or turn or anything else. It refused to come out again into the bargain. She tugged at it, pulled at it, twisted at it in exasperation, then fell over as it suddenly jerked free.

She got up quickly, hopeful something had happened to the lock, but the door still wouldn't open. In a minute she realised the screw had simply broken off in the lock, and was jammed there.

. . .

Aldan had brushed past the three waiting for the lift without really seeing them. They were simply people. People who might possibly remember a man leaving the lift later on. That didn't matter a scrap. In a place this size men were coming and going all the time. They hadn't so much as looked at him. Even if they had, if they later described him, it wouldn't matter.

You didn't go searching for anyone when there had been a terrible accident.

The cleaning woman had gone now, and the corridor carpet was clean and deserted.

He went back to Isobel's door, stood there, palming the strip of card into his right hand again, flicking his gaze left and right, listening.

Carefully he slid the card between jamb and lock tongue. He had to do it twice. And again, before it was finally in place so he could manipulate it properly. He stood there, limp with gratitude that he'd done it, then gave a sudden quick jerk of his hand. There was a click, then his left hand turned the handle.

The door swung open. He went in, footsteps soft on the wine red carpeting of the hall, closing the door gently behind him, standing there, willing himself to go on into the living room and see Isobel sprawled there in death.

CHAPTER FIFTEEN

They were suddenly almost hysterically gay, all talking at once, hardly listening to one another, almost falling over one another in their eagerness to prepare for this party that had been offered to them out of the blue.

Leaderbee was saying excitedly, "I can't manage a saucepan, but I can lay a table. If I take it slow I can lay it without a spot of trouble. Where're your dishes, young fellow?" and Leigh wasn't answering, but was saying excitedly, "The blasted bird isn't thawed. How long are you supposed to thaw the beastly things, Megan? There are chicken joints, though. Should we have those instead and save the whole bird for tonight?"

She wasn't answering him either. She was saying in an eager undertone, "The old couple at my place were going to have a duck. I know because the old lady was in the shop buying it when I went in for a little cooked chicken. And do you know, she never even spoke to me. Just nodded and moved on. Maybe she was afraid I'd see the duck and want to invite myself for dinner. And do you know," she added shamelessly, "I damned well would have, I think!"

When Leigh offered her a drink from the newly opened bottle she said in faint amazement, "Is this the first one I've had? Honestly? I feel absolutely tizzy, Leigh."

"Did you have any breakfast?"

"Good lord, I don't know. How many years ago was that? Years and years and years ago when I was hating Christmas. That's when it was!" She laughed up at him, then sobered, "Leigh, did you mean that? Did you say something about us having the whole chicken for a party tonight?"

"Yes." He looked vaguely surprised, as though the question had been settled ages ago. "You're staying of course," he added, as though the matter was finalised.

We're both half drunk, she thought in confusion. Half drunk on happiness. It's the most heady wine in the world. She was glad that Leaderbee broke across her thoughts and her talk with Leigh. She needed, she realised with a faint grin of amusement at herself, a good dose of fresh air before she disgraced herself and started to dance on the table amongst the Christmas fruit and nuts.

A nut amongst the nuts, she thought, and was so overcome at the ridiculous joke she turned away so they wouldn't see her face, going to the window, sliding it aside as far as it would go.

Fresh air, a brisk wind, touched her flushed cheeks. She closed her eyes, drawing in long breaths, knowing it was blowing over the harbour. She could smell salt in it. It was wonderful, sobering her a little.

She opened her eyes, staring in amazement.

She cried out, "Look! They were in after all! Oh Leigh, isn't that old woman a stinker! She wouldn't open for us. Look, the little girl's there. Waving again."

Leigh's hand touched hers, lay over hers on the window sill. The intoxicating happiness came welling back. She wanted to press her body back against his own. Instead she leaned forward, waving to the child.

Behind them Leaderbee said, half apologetically, "Y'know, this lady's probably got her turkey on. And pudding and that sort of thing. She wouldn't be able to be bothered with visitors right now. It's not surprising she didn't open to us. Later on maybe . . ."

"Why of course, you're perfectly right." Megan turned, flashing him a smile. "I wonder how many turkeys are cooking in this place right this minute? Just the same, I would have liked the child to have the squirrel. Later on she'll be tired. She'll probably be made to rest. We won't be welcome then, either."

Regret touched her, sharply.

Leigh said abruptly, "We could phone. I thought about it last night when she was waving then, but I thought how odd it might sound for a man to ring a child—this Miss

Tarks might have objected, thought I was trying to thrust myself on them..."

"Oh yes," her mouth and eyes mocked the conventions, "I understand."

"But *you* can ring," he pointed out. "There are three of us. She's waved to us all. The three of us..."

They went almost in a huddle to the phone, Megan and the old man pressing either side of the big nosed young man as he found the number and dialled, then silently handed the receiver to Megan.

. . .

He had never realised it was going to be so difficult, almost impossible, to force himself to go forward. He had a horrible fear that when he looked down Isobel's eyes would be open and her mouth would twist and spawn words of hate at him.

He had reminded himself that if he could have overlooked the child, he might have made a mistake about Isobel. She might have been faking death; might later have lain there, too weak to move...

Railing at himself he told himself it was impossible. He walked on, sweating, and let out a long sigh.

How absurdly peaceful she looked. How utterly peaceful. It was as though she had lain down on the fluffy white sheepskin rug for a rest. Her face was pillowed on one outflung arm. The other arm was curled against her side. Her legs lay slack, at ease, too.

He said, that horror rising in him again, "Is?" in a little questioning whisper, but the dark head didn't lift, or the curled-up body move.

A little bubbling sound of relief, of laughter against himself, welled in his throat, then was shocked into silence at the shrill sound of the telephone.

Shrill, but muffled, he realised.

He looked wildly around, searching for the instrument, not finding it, realising in astonishment the sound came from the kitchen. Had come, he realised. It had abruptly stopped.

When he went to the door he could hear the voice inside the other room as a mutter of sound.

But it was impossible, he told himself frantically. Impossible. If the child had the phone in there, why hadn't she called for help?

Because she didn't know how to use it.

The answer came with stunning force. She didn't know what numbers to dial to get help and ... yes, his gaze flicked back to the hall—the main phone was there, and a directory. The child wouldn't have another in there. She hadn't known how to dial.

But now ... the phone had rung ... and she'd answered, was speaking, and telling, explaining ...

He was moving backwards, not daring to wait. He went out, not caring how much noise he made now, letting the front door swing shut behind him, running, pressing the lift bell and then not waiting for it, hurrying to the stairway at the far end of the corridor, running downwards, frantically seeking escape.

. . .

This time she wasn't going to make a mistake. Virginia promised herself that. Before she had been so overwhelmed by the idea there was someone to talk to that she'd bungled things. This time it was different. She stopped her first headlong rush to the phone and stood there, counting to ten. Then slowly she went forward again, lifted the receiver and said, clearly, making sure there would be no mistake about anything, "This is Virginia."

A woman's voice said, "Virginia? Is that your name? Are you our little friend in the window?"

She blinked, hesitated, and the voice said again, "We're all here, Virginia. The man who decorated the tree for you, and myself and Mr. Leaderbee—we waved to you from the big tree down in the court."

Virginia forced herself not to break in, to be sensible and

wait her turn and then speak carefully and clearly as the voice went on, "We rang to wish you a very, very happy Christmas, Virginia. *Are* you happy, Virginia?"

The question was a surprise. Such a surprise her careful control broke. She blurted out, "No, no. How could I be? Please come and let me out. Let me *out*! I'm locked in here. I wasn't waving for fun. I wanted you to come and let me out. Didn't you *know*? Please come and let me out..."

They *had* to understand, she thought frantically. They mustn't hang up as daddy had done or Mr. Robbins. They had to understand.

And they did.

The woman was saying rapidly, "Dear Virginia, don't panic! We'll come and let you out. Don't panic, dear. We'll come. I promise," and then the phone was silent.

Virginia was crying great gulping tears of relief. Silly, she told herself. Silly, silly old Virginia. Silly to cry when it was now all right.

. . .

Megan's face was white. She said, "That man ... that caretaker. He'd have a master key, wouldn't he? Leigh, what can have happened over there? Where's the woman?"

He didn't answer. He was frowning at the opposite wall. Impatiently she shook at his arm. After a minute he said, "I'll ring him."

He knew he didn't want to do it. He remembered the crystal bowl, in two fragments, and Robbins gloating over what would happen. Megan was thinking of an accident, he knew, but that wasn't feasible. The child could have walked out of the flat easily if she'd been free to reach the front door.

She couldn't be, that was all. She was locked up, which meant *someone* had locked her up, in one room, or she'd accidentally locked herself in. The latter idea wasn't feasible either. Not with the woman around.

He thought of Robbins saying, "That one'd put possessions ahead of people any time"; heard him again saying, "Oh, she'll catch it when the old girl finds out".

He was afraid of what he was going to hear, he knew.

Robbins put the fear into plain words. He said crisply, "Oh yeah, sure she's locked up right enough, Mr. Warner. She's a holy terror that blasted kid. They've had a string of dailies and live-in helps in that place. None of them could put up with her. They used to have to shut her up in one of the rooms or lock her right out of the flat to get some peace. I've had them down here telling me about it.

"You saw that broken glass last night, didn't you? I told you then the old tartar'd have a fit when she found out about it. Well she's having it, that's all. She's locked the blasted kid up for punishment.

"Oh yes, she was at me a while back. I went out to sweep up and to give me hell she started throwing newspapers at me! That's what she's like. Laughing at me she was, and tossing newspapers to make me wild. She was hoping I'd go up and make a scene so the old woman would have to unlock her.

"Well she didn't get her way that was all, see. I rang up and told her I knew why she was locked in—I knew about her bustin' that bowl. You should have heard her yelp with fright when I said I had the pieces to show Miss Tarks.

"'n then later on, she was waving and yelling at a fellow in the court. He thought she was in trouble and was turning field glasses on her. I used them myself. You ought've seen her face! Talk about temper. If we'd been a bit closer and she'd had rocks she'd have tossed those at us.

"Oh, she's a sorry pest, all right, Mr. Warner. A real scorcher."

Leigh said slowly, "Surely to lock up a child, today, Christmas Day . . ."

Robbins said curtly, "You aiming on telling Miss Tarks she's a bit of a cow? You'll be told it's none of your business. She wouldn't be far out there either, would she now?"

. . .

Megan said violently, "But it's abominable! I don't care what she's done. It's Christmas Day. No one who loved a child would..."

"But Miss Tarks doesn't love her, Megan," Leigh corrected quietly. He was as disturbed as herself. The gloss, the excitement, the intoxicated happiness had suddenly gone out of the day for him. All he could think about was the child.

He said impatiently, willing her to believe it, trying to convince himself it was so, "She's a holy terror. Robbins says so."

"Robbins..." she moved impatiently, "I think he's a bit of a holy terror himself. He was abominable to Mr. Leaderbee. With no just cause..."

Leaderbee put in heavily, "Ah, that's wrong now. I was dirtying up his courtyard. He had his rights. I was in the wrong. You can't get past that."

Megan shrugged it aside, insisting, "She must be terribly upset and frightened..."

"Did she sound frightened?" Leigh put in sharply. "You know she didn't, Megan. She sounded quite placid, till she lost her temper and started to demand we do something about letting her out. She wasn't frightened when she threw newspapers at Robbins and laughed at him. You must admit, Megan, she *does* sound a bit of a terror."

"It's no way to treat a child," she persisted.

"Perhaps not..."

"And she's such a friendly little thing. Leigh, I don't believe she's a little horror. If she is it's probably these women ... the dailies and live-in helps Robbins talks about—they've made her afraid of people, of ... she *is* friendly, Leigh. She was waving..." she stopped, remembering now that the child had upbraided her impatiently, asking why they hadn't guessed she wasn't playing a game, but was demanding they come and let her out.

She said sharply, "Last night it *was* a game. She was happy."

"Last night," he reminded, equally sharply, "she hadn't

been found out. Miss Tarks didn't know about the broken crystal. Now she does. Virginia isn't happy any more, as she admitted to you, but . . . I'm afraid she brought it on herself. Oh no, Megan," she saw his head shake firmly, "we can't interfere. We'd get a tongue-blistering if we went round now and demanded the woman let her out. She wouldn't do it, and she'd tell us off. As Robbins said, it isn't our business."

He went on coaxingly, trying to bring back the intoxication of happiness to her eyes, "Later tonight, if we see her at the window we can wave, and ring again and ask if she's happy then, and then go around . . ."

She shook her head. Her eyes seemed enormous, lost-looking in grief. "Don't you see—we've failed her. We promised to help and now we're not going to. She won't forgive us. She won't want to see us or speak to us. We made a promise and we broke it and failed her. A child doesn't forgive that."

CHAPTER SIXTEEN

How slow they were, Virginia thought restlessly. Impossibly slow, really. She was sure the clock had stopped. The hands hadn't seemed to alter for ages, and ages, but she knew it was a terribly long time since the phone call and the promise.

They'd promised, she reminded. The woman had said there were three of them—herself and someone called Mr. Leaderbee—and what a funny name that was, she reflected idly—and there was the man who'd trimmed the tree, too.

They weren't the sort of people who broke a promise. They weren't housekeepers or daily women or Lady Help people. She was quite convinced of it. Last night they'd all played together.

Now they'd made her a promise.

If only they'd hurry...

She thought anxiously, but they can't get in without a key. They must be talking to Mr. Robbins now.

She was frightened again, thinking of Robbins. What was he saying to them, she wondered frantically. Was he telling them she'd broken that glass bowl and was locked up for punishment?

But they wouldn't listen. She shook her head vehemently at the idea. They'd say, "But Virginia's a nice little girl. She shouldn't be locked up that way Mr. Robbins, so even if she's been naughty we want you to let her out and ... and have her come and have Christmas dinner with us."

That flight of imagination was consolation and balm. She went on dwelling on the idea, adding to it, building up a wonderful picture of herself as the centre of attention in the kind man's flat. There'd be turkey and pudding and crackers and icecream and balloons, she was sure.

Everyone would be terribly sorry for her, locked up like

that. They'd even, she thought happily, put patches on Miss Tarks and make her sit up and drink a glass of Christmas wine, so even that particular unpleasantness would be solved.

It was going to be marvellous, she reflected.

But after a while she knew far too much time had gone. Slowly she went over to the window, gazing out, searching for watching faces, upbraiding herself for not doing that before, for not realising the three people ... not three she amended ... because someone would be talking to Robbins ... but one or two would be gazing out the window, waving to her crying, "Just a little minute longer, Virginia. Just a tiny minute more, so be brave, won't you?"

She leaned out, staring across the court. The window was blank. Different. She realised suddenly that the looped back curtains had had their loops undone. They were lying right across the window.

"Go away, Virginia," the curtains seemed to say. "The people here don't want to see you any more, or see you wave. They're not waving any more either. The curtains have been closed to shut you and your pleas out from sight."

She stared in panic, then rage.

It was Robbins, she knew that quite well. He'd told them about the bowl and her being shut up and they'd believed it, and they ... oh horrible thought! ... they didn't care. They'd gone back to their home and pulled the curtains so they shouldn't see her any more.

They wouldn't ring either, so she could explain. Oh, why hadn't she explained before? But they'd asked if she was happy and she'd said no and told them to come and get her out and there'd been no time, or even need so it had seemed then. They'd seemed to understand.

And they'd promised.

She couldn't get over that—over the promise that had been made and was broken.

She leaned out. She screamed to the closed curtains, "You promised! You promised!" but they didn't slide apart, and her voice was caught by the wind, carried away and drowned from hearing by sounds coming from other windows all round the court.

. . .

Aldan saw the small figure. With his glasses he could see her face. It was filled with anguish now, and she was crying out, waving, but though he scanned every window overlooking the court, there wasn't anyone watching or anyone to hear her.

But he didn't dare go back. She'd spoken to someone. By now that someone must be travelling towards her, or had summoned the police, or was ringing the caretaker...

The caretaker, he remembered, had thought the child was locked up for misbehaviour, but what was he going to do when he learned Isobel was dead...

He frowned. He realised that the child couldn't know that and couldn't have told anyone. She couldn't have seen through the locked door. At the most she would have heard the shot and wouldn't, surely, have known what it was.

She couldn't possibly have known what had happened. She could only have said to that caller, "I'm locked in and can't make Miss Tarks hear."

What was that going to sound like?

Punishment, he thought in satisfaction.

He didn't believe now that the police would come. If the caller had thought there was real trouble the police would have arrived long ago. There was still the thought to be fought with, that the caller was on the way, or was talking to the caretaker ... that someone would soon arrive at the flat.

He didn't dare go back for fear he was trapped up there, but he didn't dare leave either. Till he knew what was going to happen. He went on standing in the shadow of the tree, watching.

. . .

It was all Robbins' fault. She hated him. Oh how she hated him! Virginia raged round the tiny room, her small fists clenched, her face red with anguished fury.

She opened the rubbish chute, crying down it, "I hate you, I hate you!" even though she was certain he couldn't hear.

She thought again of sending down a message. It seemed the only thing left to do. She went back to the cupboard and fetched out the newspapers, scattering them, selecting a big sheet from a morning daily. There wasn't much red colouring left in the small bottle, but she managed to scrawl big letters all over the paper page.

"Let me out," they demanded.

She couldn't write any more because the red colour ran out. In any case she was quite aware she didn't know how to print or spell all the words that would have been necessary to say what was wrong, and it would have taken sheets and sheets of paper into the bargain, because her straggling wobbly letters filled almost the whole sheet.

She went back to the chute and let the uncreased paper slide into dimness.

She thought in sudden confident hope, "He'll see now. He'll know I must be in the kitchen, and you don't lock bad girls up in kitchens. They can break things. And you can't cook your dinner or make yourself a cup of tea. Oh, he'll see *now*. He'll know something's wrong and he'll look so silly when he comes and finds Miss Tarks and me."

. . .

Leaderbee was explaining, "You see, miss, that young doc was quite wrong. When I put my thinking cap on I could see how to do it—sew two towels together and get one big long one, then jiggle it under my feet and rub, holding each end, without bending. You can dry your feet that way without bending at all. Just shows you.

"I should have thought of it long ago, then I wouldn't have burned my feet. You see I couldn't manage and I stuck them in front of the radiator and next thing I went off to sleep. Woke up with them done to a turn as you might say, though no real harm done. I healed up well, but you should have heard that young doctor telling me I wasn't safe on my own."

Megan said abstractedly, her mind still half on the flat across the court, "Wouldn't you feel safer, happier in..." then stopped.

"A home?" he suggested sadly. "The doc said that, too, but no, I wouldn't. I can manage quite well and my home's been my own for thirty years. I'd miss it too much. I can still plant a few flowers in my own garden, too. They don't need much care. Flowers always come up sweet as you please without trouble for me. It's just a kind of gift. And then ... I've plenty of time, you see. I can take all the time I like in doing things. You want to come and see my house, miss. I can still do a bit of painting, and all my housework and so on. It's just cooking—handling heavy things, you see, because my hands shake. Just old age, the doc said. There's naught else wrong with my health." He gave her a cheeky grin, "I'm just slowly wearing out like an old clock."

"Haven't you ever thought of getting a woman in to cook? I mean, if she had a couple of rooms..."

He gave a wry chuckle. "I tried it and would you believe in a month she was hinting we'd do better being married. At my age, mind you! I'm not so silly I didn't know she was after my furniture and bit of cash in the bank. I tried again and nearly got bossed out of my own house. She used to shoot me outside like an old dog—almost locking me out while she cleaned and cooked." He drew in his breath sharply. "You know, I can tell just how that little 'un across the court feels."

He rose slowly to his feet, "Would you mind," he was looking at them both apologetically, "if I nicked down and had a breath of air? I can see I can't help and a bit of a walk before eating helps the digestion, if you follow me."

He went with apparent casualness, but once on the ground floor and out of the lift, his legs went faster. He'd agreed straight away that there'd be no more waving or looking out at the child—no encouragement to her at all. It was the right thing to do, he knew quite well, but for the life of him he couldn't bear to think of her shut up like that, unwanted, on Christmas Day.

He was going to go back to the tree and look up. He might risk a wave if she was there. He'd stand in the court, he decided, and shake his head to tell her there was nothing doing about her getting out of her punishment. But he'd wave, too, to show her *he* wasn't cross, that she still had a friend, though there wasn't a thing he could do to help her.

He was panting as he entered the courtyard. Disappointment welled over him as he saw the place was occupied already. He hesitated, knowing he was going to look a pretty fool standing in the court and shaking his head and waving. He nearly turned on his heel and went away again. Then he caught sight of the child.

He squinted his eyes in alarm at the way she was leaning out. That was dangerous, he reflected in real anxiety. The woman up there should be ashamed. Didn't she realise that a little child might take risks to get help on Christmas Day, and lean out too far?

Turning sharply he saw the other fellow just turning away. He'd known though, that the man had been watching himself watch the child. He had felt the man's gaze on his bent back.

He said shakily, "That's real dangerous, wouldn't you say, sir? Wouldn't you say that woman ought to be ashamed of herself? On Christmas Day, too. That isn't fair. Is it?"

The man only half turned. He asked brusquely, "What isn't? What woman? That's a child. Your eyes must be bad."

"They aren't, then. I knew it was a child," Leaderbee protested. "A little girl. Her name's Virginia. She's a friend of mine, see. Why, I was just speaking to her on the phone a while back. I know all about it, you see."

He drew a breath of satisfaction. He had the fellow's attention now and it was a relief to talk and not have the young fellow upstairs telling him it wasn't any good thinking about it any more.

He went over to the bench and sat down, hoping the other fellow would come and sit down too so they could have a real gossip, but the man went on standing still, seeming to gaze at the tree.

"What do you know about?" he asked suddenly. So suddenly that Leaderbee positively jumped.

"Eh?" He stared in bewilderment.

The answer came impatiently, "You said something about speaking to the child and knowing all about it. About what?"

"Ah, that was what I was going to tell you, see. We were going round to see her. We'd had a game with her, waving to her from down here and the young fellow's window, that side," he pointed. "We thought we'd go round and say Merry Christmas and give her a bit of a present, but the old woman in there with her wouldn't open the door.

"Oh well," he nodded wisely, "she was probably busy, but we were disappointed, so we thought we'd ring her up. The little girl, that is. So we did. Just now, a little while back. It was the little girl answered.

"She told us her name was Virginia and that she wasn't happy. We asked if she was, see. And then she said she was locked up and to please come and get her out." He sighed. "We didn't understand, see. We thought there was some sort of trouble. So we promised we'd come and let her out. At once.

"But it wasn't what we'd thought. We got onto the caretaker to tell him to come along and do something and he told us the little girl was locked up for being naughty."

He went on speaking, telling the silent stranger all about the glass bowl, and the thrown newspapers and Virginia's temper.

When he stopped the man asked, "Did you ring back and tell her you weren't coming?"

Leaderbee shuffled uneasily ."No," he admitted ruefully. "Mind you the young chap is right. She must know she's getting punished and that we'd find out fast enough. We can't go interfering. Anyway the old woman wouldn't listen to us. As young Warner says we just should let the curtains go across our window and not look out at her any more— just ignore her.

"Ah, he's right, of course, but I couldn't . . . I just wanted to try and make her understand I was sorry, even though I couldn't help." He squinted his gaze upwards. "But I see she's gone inside again. Maybe," he suggested hopefully, "the old lady has unlocked the door now."

"Most probably. She wouldn't lock her up all day. I wouldn't worry."

Leaderbee watched the man walk briskly away. After a while, after another glance at the window, Leaderbee rose too and walked slowly back inside to the lift.

. . .

Aldan now was furious with himself for his flight. If he'd only had the simple guts to wait for a while, he upbraided himself, he wouldn't now have the whole job to do again. He still had to get back inside the flat. But at least now there'd be no one about when he threw the child out. He'd wait till everyone was at their Christmas dinner, and now he could count on not even the young fellow across the court happening to look out to see what the child was doing.

It was incredible how everything was adding up to help him. There was the caretaker, fobbing away all suspicion; there was the old chap who'd seen the child leaning out dangerously; there was the fact it was Christmas Day and her cries and waves were being mistaken for a game.

Confidently he moved towards the lift, entered it, heard the doors whisper as they closed.

Equally confidently he pressed the button for the sixth floor.

. . .

Virginia's delighted little dance stopped. She was alarmed, dismayed again.

For a minute she had been able to think of nothing except Robbins jumping up out of a chair down in the basement and picking up her note as it fell and saying to himself, "She must be in the kitchen. But that's all wrong. How's Miss Tarks going to cook the dinner if she's locked up the child in the kitchen?"

But now she was thinking of Robbins, not in the basement watching papers falling down the chute, but in his kitchen, cooking an enormous turkey.

It might be hours and hours, she thought in horror, before he looked again into the basement and by then ... she thought of all the other turkeys busily cooking all over the building, thought of all the bones and scraps to be wrapped up very soon and whisked away down the garbage chutes. She could picture them falling one by one, on top of her notice, covering it completely.

She saw Robbins refusing to work because it was a holiday. She saw him putting on his best suit and going out to visit his mother, a bunch of flowers in his rough hand. She saw him coming back after dark and falling straight into bed, while all the time vast parcels of rubbish came falling down the chutes all over the building, piling up and over her notice.

"What am I going to do?" she asked the silent clock. She couldn't even look through the keyhole now, to see if the foot had moved, because the screw was still jammed in the hole. She couldn't ring the three people who'd waved to her because she didn't know how to get hold of them on the telephone.

Pensively she eyed the instrument. She wondered what would happen if she just stuck her fingers in the holes of the dial and spun it round and round. Would someone answer her?

. . .

Again, he thought and the fury of disappointment was so violent he could have run from the lift and caught her, smashed his fist into her face and toppled her backwards, right down to the end of the corridor, finishing the job with a thrust of her body down the stairs.

He recognised the face when she turned. Even though it was now carefully made up and the fluffy pink duster had given place to carefully waved hair, and the bolster-like pink robe had changed to a gay print dress, he recognised her by the voice that cried, seeing him there, with the lift doors whispering behind him, "There you are! Did you tell her? Or isn't she home?"

She came hurrying towards him, teetering a little on absurdly high heels. "When she didn't ring up or anything I thought either you hadn't told her or she was so darn wild with us she wasn't going to answer. I've been ringing, but there's no answer. Isn't she home? Have you come back again to see..."

He didn't know what to say. He burst out at last, "How should I know whether she's home? I went away. I haven't tried the bell yet."

She said archly, "But I have. You can take my word for it she's not home. I leaned out my window a while back to sniff the air. There's not a trace of dinner cooking coming from her place. I'm sure of it. She's out. Isn't that a disappointment for you." She was eyeing his fieldglasses in their case, "Are you down for the day? Just to see her? From the country perhaps?"

He could cheerfully have hit, and continued to hit at her till the arch smile and the tinny high voice were gone. Instead he said, "I'm staying in the district. I was... just looking her up. It doesn't matter."

"Oh but it does." Red taloned hands touched his arm, pulling at him. He wanted to strike at the two hands clasping round the grey sleeve of his coat. Instead he remained rigidly still as she cried, "Never mind, you can drown your disappointment in a drink before you go. Oh no, don't say no! You couldn't, not today! Just one drink... somehow it will make me feel better. About last night you know. You're a friend of hers—I'll feel I'm someway making amends... oh come on, you can't say no!"

It was better to go, he thought wearily. Where was the harm in it? They weren't likely to mention him later. Even if they did what was there to say—merely that an old friend called and couldn't get in.

Excitement touched him again. There it was again—luck helping him. This was helping him, not hindering him at all. Funny he hadn't seen that at once. Later, if he was mentioned, the woman would say how disappointed he'd been, how he'd come twice but . . . had never gone in.

She'd say so, and it would be taken for the truth.

The flat was in half darkness, too. She apologised for that, babbling something about Rog's head being bad and the light hurting his eyes. She wanted to pull one of the blinds up, but he stopped her, managed a laugh, told her his own head wasn't too good for that matter.

She screamed with laughter, reminding him horribly of Greta's ghastly amusement. The glass she gave him was slippery. He knew it hadn't been washed. He could see a litter of glasses on a side table and knew it had come from there and was disgusted, even while he made himself drink the stuff. It was warm, too weak, and as disgusting as the glass.

Even then she wouldn't let him go. She flitted between kitchen and the living room, telling him that Rog, whoever that was, would be up soon, and to stay and have a drink with him.

He told her, glancing at his watch, he could stay another five minutes. He had an appointment. For Christmas dinner. That got him out of any possible invitation to stay and share hers, he thought complacently. He told her he'd merely dropped back again on his way to see if Miss Tarks was back, meaning to say only Merry Christmas and go.

Listening to her using up the five minutes in inane chatter, he was thinking only that everything in this day was helping him to safety.

. . .

Virginia was wrong. When she had been picturing him basting a huge turkey in the most gigantic of roasting pans, Robbins was in the basement.

The boiler was the only companion he had for Christmas. In his present morose mood he considered it a better one than human company.

He looked at it almost with affection as he undid the clips holding the rubbish collection bag to its stand.

At intervals through each day he set aside the partly filled bags and replaced them with a fresh one. With satisfaction he saw the present bag was nearly full of bottles. That meant dollars and cents in his pockets as soon as he got rid of them. A lot of them, he saw with further satisfaction, were soft drink ones. Amazing the way people tossed them down, as though three cents deposit was a trifle and not to be bothered about.

He was fixing the new bag into the stand when the first parcel of rubbish came down, falling with a dull little thud at the bottom of the empty sack. It was followed soon after, as he set the final clip into place, by a single sheet of newspaper.

For a minute he thought it was covered with blood and he wrinkled his nose in disgust, thinking it had been round some turkey's neck. They were a disgusting lot, he thought, the way they threw down papers like that without wrapping a bit more round them. Sometimes he got his hands covered with all sorts of muck that nearly turned his stomach.

He peered down. No, no blood he realised. He hooked the sheet out with the long, steel tipped stick he used on the bags.

For a minute he stared, then grinned.

"Well, you're a cool one," he turned and surveyed the wide mouth of the chute that led away, up through the brick walls of the building, into smaller and smaller passages that finished in kitchen chute panels. "You're a cool one," he said to the chute. "A clever little one, too."

Honestly, he thought, spreading the paper out and putting it under the crystal bowl, you couldn't help laughing at her. Oh yes, she was a clever one. He wondered if sound carried up the chute so she'd heard him down here fixing the bags, choosing her time to a nicety.

It didn't matter. But he'd show it to Miss Tarks he promised himself. He'd show her and say, "See what I have to put with up with. She throws newspapers at me in the court, and messages at me down the chute, trying to scare me half to death and she scowls at me and yells at me ... oh dear, she's a one, that one."

Yawning, already forgetting her, he decided he might as well start getting his dinner. Then he'd have a nap.

. . .

At first there was only a series of clicks and rattles and squawks. It faintly amused her at first, but as time went on it irritated her.

Impatiently she jiggled the key as she had seen her schoolteacher do once, then she slipped a small finger into the dial holes again and patiently dialled.

She was utterly astonished when music came out of the black receiver, and over it a man's voice burst out, with surprising loudness, "Hullo, hullo there. Merry Christmas and all that. Hullo?"

"This ... this is Virginia," she gulped.

There was a roar of laughter. The voice said, "Well, well, Virginia? Oh yes, Virginia, there *is* a Santa Claus."

"I never said anything about Santa Claus," she gulped in astonishment. "I never ... I ... I ... I want you to come and open the door. Please come and ..."

The laughter brayed in her ear. "Virginia? Hey!" the voice seemed as though it had gone a little distance away, "Any of you chaps know a Virginia? You, Ted? Well she's downstairs anyway—must be at the call box on the corner. Wants us to open the door ..."

A voice yelled back, "Holy cow, is that front bell busted again! Tell her to come on ... I can't remember her, but never mind, the more the merrier. Tell her to come on and I'll go down ..."

"Please ..." she was calling desperately, "I wanted you to come and ..."

"Right, sweetheart," the voice brayed. "We're coming. Meet you at the door, so purse up your pretty lips for a kiss."

Virginia said solemnly to the silent phone, "I think people are *mad*."

CHAPTER SEVENTEEN

Leigh was asking, "Megan haven't you anyone? Not even in another state, or town? I've a sister at least, and a nephew. He's three years old. They're camping in Sorrento, down in Victoria."

"I suppose there are some relations somewhere," she answered vaguely. "I haven't seen any of my father's people for donkey's years. He died when I was five. They just drifted away from us. We didn't seem to belong to that side of the family any more. You can't blame them, I expect.

"I know my mother had lots of cousins, too. They drifted away, married, went overseas, that sort of thing. I suppose if I tried hard enough I could trace a lot of them."

"By your dubious expression you consider they'd prove to have two heads, at least."

She burst out laughing, then sobered to say, "I've never been able to understand why one should prefer relatives to friends. Often the first are terrible and the last are wonderful."

"Have you many friends, Megan?"

She surveyed him levelly, asked candidly, "Does it seem like it? I did once. They got married. Once that happens you're odd one out."

Leaderbee was surveying the pair of them with interest. "That's it, miss. You lose one set of friends when you marry and get another set—other married pairs. Then next thing you know you're a widower, or widow, as may be, and bless me you've lost another lot. You're a single again and you don't fit.

"Trouble is, when you're *my* age, you don't fancy marrying again and starting things round for a second go. Else I might have taken up with that woman I had to come in and cook. She was a good cook," he sighed.

"So am I," Megan told him. "Maybe I'd better come and cook for you, Mr. Leaderbee."

He drew a sharp breath. Don't be a fool, he told himself, and in the same breath told himself he'd be a fool if he didn't do what he wanted. There was so much that was queer and uncanny and downright upside down about this day that a bit more wouldn't hurt, for a certainty.

He said briskly, "Righto, miss, how about it? Now look... you listen a bit. I've got this house. I rent it mind, but the landlord can't get me out, so why worry. I'm set so long as I pay up, till they carry me out on my back. You could have a couple of rooms all to yourself and your friends. Nicely furnished, too. And clean. I swear to that. You can have them for nothing, for doing my cooking. How about it?"

When she didn't answer he sighed. He'd put his foot in it, he thought helplessly. Now she was annoyed. But she'd said, hadn't she, how she hated her present place and felt she was living with ghosts? Well, he wasn't a ghost.

He said, brightness returning to his eyes, "I don't act like a ghost, Miss Megan. I sing in my bath. Or try to. And I talk to the flowers. I bang doors, too. I tramp mud on the floors. I have a bath any old hour and not by a sort of military roster. And..." He thought around for something completely unghostlike, "And I snore and make noises drinking soup!" he finished triumphantly.

The three of them were suddenly laughing helplessly. Between gusts of laughter Leaderbee gurgled, "Oh what a day we're having—what a game! Wouldn't the little 'un over the way love to join in with us..."

They were suddenly silent, eyes avoiding other eyes.

Abruptly, defiantly, Megan went to the window and pulled back one of the curtains, looking out. She swung round. She said violently, "Leigh, we've got to do something. It's abominable. She's there at the window. By herself. Locked in on Christmas Day. Alone."

. . .

What else could she do, Virginia wondered, debating whether to try the phone again or not. She dreaded getting the stupid man with his talk of Santa Claus. He had vaguely frightened her. Uneasily she drifted to the window, hoping the curtains across the way would have been pulled back, or someone else was looking out.

For one moment she thought she saw the curtain shift, and she went eagerly to the sill, but when it didn't draw right back, when no one looked out and waved to her, she drifted back, thumb knuckle to her mouth, to the phone, lifting the receiver again, hopefully, wearily beginning to spin the dial once more.

. . .

Safety, Aldan thought. Safety only a short distance, a short time, a short effort away. He stood against Isobel's door again, knowing the woman in the flat next door was safely occupied now with her cooking; aware that with the lowered blinds she wouldn't so much as see the child fall and come racing out to crash into him as he left Isobel's flat when it was all over.

He almost laughed at the reflection that even Rog's aching head was the means of another measure of safety for himself.

Because luck seemed so much on his side, he was utterly, completely, astonished that the card didn't slide into position with his first effort. Being baulked over such a trifle made him tense and angry, so that he had to keep trying over and over.

He had to try seven times before finally he had the card into place. Seven times lucky, he thought then, the tenseness going. It returned though when again he stood in the little hallway. It was just as it had been before. He had to force himself into every step forward, which was ridiculous, because he'd seen Isobel before, knew she was really dead, knew that there was nothing horrible about the scene, nothing revolting, or stomach churning.

He still had to use force with every footstep he took and when he finally stood in the doorway, looking down at her, he found himself frantically wondering if she hadn't moved—if the head wasn't slightly more on her left cheek, if her curled up arm wasn't relaxed ever so slightly.

He said questioningly, as he'd said that other time, "Is?" as though she might wake at his voice and raise her head, and speak to him.

Finally he managed to walk on, so that his steps passed her head, her waist, her hips, her knees, her feet.

He stood then, unable to move, unable to turn, terrified that if he did he'd find she'd played a trick on him, and had let him pass, only to rise up behind him, to wait till he turned and saw her grinning.

He swung round in one violent movement.

There was no trick, no Isobel watching him.

He shook his head, trying to clear it of any imaginings at all, trying to concentrate on the job that lay ahead.

He turned, kneeling, sliding his head against her still body, into the pocket of her apron, feeling his fingers close round the key there. He stood up and instantly almost forgot she was there at all.

Gently he palmed the key, moving it towards the lock, meaning to ease it in and softly turn it so the child wouldn't hear him coming till too late.

When the key didn't slide in at the first try he simply tried again. And again. Then slowly, still making no noise, he bent and peered into the keyhole.

Something was jammed into it he could see, but whatever it was he intended the key to poke it out and confidently he thrust the key forward.

It simply refused to go in. Cursing softly he rocked back on his heels, considering it, trying again to see into the hole and find out exactly what it was. He could guess the child must have tried getting out and merely succeeded in jamming the lock, but what had she used?

He considered the matter again, moved from a hunched

up position on his heels, to his bent knees, kneeling there by the door.

He remembered the old man speaking of her mentioning her name.

He tapped softly on the panels. He called, "Virginia."

CHAPTER EIGHTEEN

Megan said, "I don't care, I know everything you're saying is reasonable. I know it isn't my business and that I'll probably get the door slammed in my face. I don't care. I'm still going up there and I'm going to ring and knock till that woman opens up and then I'm going to tell her exactly what I think of her."

Leigh leaned, cross-legged, against the sink. He looked almost bored as he asked, "What good do you think that will do? It will soothe your outraged feelings of course, but what do you think it will do to the old bird's? She'll be furious. She seems the type to kick the cat when she's furious, but she hasn't a cat. No animals allowed in this human hive. That's one of the rules. There are humpty seven more. I won't bore you with them. But she'll still want something to kick. There'll only be the child. Can't you see her calling through that locked door, "You wicked, wicked girl, Virginia. Making trouble, and calling to people, so they come here and abuse me. For that ... you can not only go without your Christmas dinner, Virginia, but your tea and your supper as well. *That* will teach you, Virginia."

In the same almost bored voice he added, "Pretty idea, isn't it, Megan," then his voice softened. "Oh Megan, Megan, you can't force the world to change because you want it to do so. Haven't you found that out, yet?" He crossed to her, lifted her downbent head by two hands either side her chin. "Cheer up, Megan. If we don't interfere there's a good chance the kid will be let free this afternoon. We can go round after our dinner and suggest we take her out. The old woman might agree just to get her off her hands for a bit. How about that?"

Her eyes brightened. She asked, "Where could we take

her?" as though it was already settled they should go.

"Well..."

Leaderbee broke in eagerly, "We could go to my place. I know that doesn't sound much, but I never told you, did I, that I used to be a magician?" He chuckled, slapping his hands on his knees, "Ah, that surprised you, didn't it? I was good at it, too, till my hands let me down, but you can't do tricks with the shakes, so I had to give up. I've got all my stuff though—trick cards and fancy get ups and all. I can tell you two how to do a few easy tricks. Teach her too. She'd love it, wouldn't you say?"

Megan was smiling at him. He heard her voice through a haze of content, "And it will give me a chance to see the rooms I'll have. Won't it, Mr. Leaderbee? Or have you decided it wouldn't work out? I'll be out at work all day. I'll only be able to cook breakfast and dinner ... and of course at the weekends..."

His smile was completely happy and content. "That'll do fine. I wouldn't expect more. And later on," he carefully didn't look at either of them, "if you find you're going to marry ... well, the chap mightn't have a home ready for you, and it might be just the thing if you stayed on there at my place—the more the merrier, it seems to me."

. . .

Virginia couldn't make up her mind which was the worst—the squawks, the silences or having the Santa Claus man back. She dreaded hearing him again, but after a while she dreaded the squawks and the silences, too. She was so tired of it all that she was nearly giving up, when she turned sharply.

She stood still, listening, gulping in panic. She had been sure, just for one minute, there'd been a sound at the locked doorway. She stood there imagining Miss Tarks, disordered hair in spikes round her head, wild-eyed, rising from the floor and drifting soundlessly towards the door, trying it, trying to get in to her guest.

Suddenly she knew she didn't want Miss Tarks in there with her—not the Miss Tarks who was there in imagination. But after a moment, when nothing more happened, the panic died. She told herself not to be silly; to give herself one more try on the phone.

Her finger was sore from dialling. She expected, when she had finished, that there'd be another squawk, but instead, after a moment, a quiet voice said, "Hullo? Valance here."

She heard it, and heard the soft knock too. Terrified, appalled that at any moment the door would fly open and Miss Tarks would stand there, crying, "Virginia, what are you doing with my phone?" she slammed the receiver down, huddling back against the wall, waiting.

The soft knock came again. And a third time. A voice, muffled, but clearly heard, called her name.

"Virginia," it called and she gave a little whimpering cry.

Then panic flowed out of her. You silly, she scolded herself. You silly Virginia. Miss Tarks has the key. She wouldn't knock and call. The key's out there in that room with her. It's someone...

It was someone to help, of course.

She ran to the door, knocking back, crying, "Let me out!"

The voice said, more loudly now, "Virginia, be quiet. Hush." and when she had obeyed it went on, "Virginia, listen to me. I know you're locked up and I've come to let you out. Can you hear me, Virginia?"

"Yes," she whispered, and repeated it more loudly.

"Good."

"Who are you? Are you the man with the tree?" she asked excitedly. Now there were no more things to worry about; no more dialling of phones or calling for help or waving or sending messages down the chute.

She was bubbling over with eagerness to question and explain. She rushed on hopefully, remembering that odd fascinating name, "Or are you Mr. Leaderbee? How old are you, Mr. Leaderbee? Couldn't you read my message on the window? Or is it you, nice man with the tree? What's *your* name? *You* read my message, didn't you, only Robbins told you lies, didn't he and..."

"Virginia," the voice broke in, "your message was all wrong."

Now that he was safely inside, he had all the time in the world, Aldan was reflecting. There was no need to hurry. He could spare time to soothe her, make her trust him, so there'd later be no trouble. He wouldn't toss her out till everyone was safely at dinner or sleeping it off afterwards. There was plenty of time. If anyone came now they'd go away thinking the flat was empty. There was nothing to worry about.

Almost lazily he explained, "Didn't you realise, Virginia, that while you could read your message on the window, it didn't say Help from the other side? People outside saw only the backs of your letters; the backs made no message at all. They didn't look like letters. They looked like ... well, squiggles and wriggles."

Virginia was astonished and suddenly highly amused.

"I just never thought," she returned through the door. "I never thought, but ... *you* knew. How clever of you," she congratulated, clapping her hands with delight. "Who are you? The man with the tree?"

He nearly said yes, then realised that when he had the door open she'd know he'd lied and be upset and perhaps start yelling and cause trouble.

He denied, "No. I don't know who you're talking about, Virginia. I don't live here in the building. I just came to look at your Christmas tree down there in the courtyard and I saw you waving and waving. Did you see me down there? I was with the caretaker?"

"Yes."

She was suddenly scowling, wondering what Robbins had said about her.

He was going on, "I was worried about you leaning out that way. Worried about that funny back-to-front message too, but Robbins told me not to worry at all, because you were locked up for being a terribly naughty girl."

"But it isn't true," she cried frantically, afraid that now he might go away again and leave her still locked up.

"Oh, I know it isn't."

He wondered why she hadn't mentioned Miss Tarks. Because she'd see the woman's body probably when the door first opened—before he could prevent her—he said deliberately, "I found Miss Tarks out here, you see, lying on the floor."

Virginia remembered. She asked, "Is she dead?"

He said, "Yes," remembering that when the child saw the body she'd want to know why he wasn't doing anything to help, if she was supposed to be merely sick or hurt. She might run to the woman, kneel beside her...

He shuddered, remaining silent, expecting questions, even tears and wails from the other side of the door, but Virginia seemed to dismiss the whole subject of Miss Tarks. He couldn't begin to understand that to Virginia finality spelt exactly that. When something happened finally, beyond any helping, there was simply no use worrying about it. You only worried about things when you had hope that the badness would go right away—things like getting out of a locked room.

She asked suddenly, "How did you get in? Did you make Mr. Robbins give you his key?"

"Yes. He wouldn't come up. He said I was crazy to worry about you and he wasn't going to spend his holiday fussing about you. I think he's rather an unpleasant fellow, don't you, Virginia?"

"He's a pig," she informed him blithely, "but *you're* not. Oh please, open the door, so I can see you," she cried eagerly "I'm sure you must look nice and..."

"But I can't open it yet, Virginia. Oh, I will in a minute. Don't worry. But you've jammed something in the lock, haven't you? The key's out here, but I can't get it into the lock at all. What have you done to it?"

For a moment she simply didn't remember. So much had happened she couldn't begin to remember what she had done. Only when she looked down and saw the tinopener where she had dropped it, did remembrance come flowing back.

She told him all about her attempt to make the lock open, and he said, "I see. Well, this may take a bit of time, Virginia. I'll have to winkle the screw out some way before I can get the key in. Do you understand? It may take time, but I'll manage it. Sit down and be a good girl till I'm through."

Virginia said with the utmost conviction, "I'll be so good you wouldn't believe."

. . .

It must have died of malnutrition, Robbins thought in disgust. It had looked bad enough when he'd unwrapped it the previous evening—although the man in the shop had sworn it was a prime grilling chicken—but now it was cooked it looked as though he was having roast sparrow. Why, he might as well have gone out into the courtyard and let fly a scatter of bird shot and picked out the plumpest bird that had fallen out of the heavens.

Thinking of that reminded him of the old coot who'd tried to have a picnic with the birds. He wished now he hadn't shooed him off. The girl had looked as though she'd willingly bite him in two. If she told the story to some of the residents and they liked to make a fuss it might be unpleasant.

He reminded himself, slipping the chicken onto a plate, that he'd only been doing his duty. That was it. His plain duty. They'd have more to complain of if he let the court be littered with crusts and bits of paper...

He wished he hadn't thought of that. It reminded him of the kid tossing newspapers at him.

When the phone rang he took a full minute debating whether to let it ride or answer it. Only the thought that it might, just possibly, be the managing agents ringing—a thing they were horribly prone to do on a holiday just to make sure he or his relief was on duty, made him lift it.

Then he swore, muttered bitterly, "old gabby gab" and listened to the soaring voice, his temper getting worse and worse all the time.

He said bitterly, "Mrs. Gilbert, what do you think I am?

How do you expect me to cope when people here let a bit of a kid strew the place with paper? That's what happened. It's that Segal kid. She spent the morning tossing newspaper out at me. I tell you I started cleaning up and then she pitched in . . . I nearly wept," he added pathetically.

It didn't do any good. She was offended by the sight. Her visitors were offended. Her husband was offended. And let him remember her husband was the friend of one of the managing agents, if he pleased.

He wasn't pleased at all, but he merely said he'd attend to the court as soon as possible and yes, he'd tell Mr. Segal the child had to be kept under control.

Oh, that was one thing he'd certainly do, he thought grimly. He'd tell Segal and he'd tell Miss Tarks, too. Now he had a real excuse for pitching into her. She'd let it happen, hadn't she, and now there were complaints. Let her face up to that.

He stuck the bird into the warming tray and went almost happily back to the phone, found the number and dialled.

. . .

In the kitchen on the sixth floor Virginia sat with folded hands. She was sorry now she had wiped grubbiness from them all over her pinafore. It looked terrible. She was sure her hair did too and possibly her face was grubby into the bargain. She was sorry about it, because she would have liked the man outside to have a good first impression of herself.

She thought how clever he was, and how stupid Robbins was in comparison and couldn't resist smiling. She and the man outside were going to tell the whole world about Robbins. The man . . .

She went to the door. She said politely, "I'm very sorry for speaking, but, would you tell me your name?"

On the other side Aldan stopped probing at the keyhole, thought, and said, "Herbert Baring," not realising that the name was an acute disappointment to her.

It was, she reflected sadly, stodgy. Like rice pudding. Not

at all the sort of name that went with cleverness and kindness.

Aldan was already forgetting what he'd told her. The lock was proving unexpectedly difficult and he was softly cursing as he worked, knowing he had to get the screw out before he could slide the lock back at all. He didn't want to damage it in any way, though if signs of the screw's passage were later evident it wouldn't really matter. Damage could have been caused at any time. It would be the handle the police would concentrate on anyway. The broken off knob on the kitchen side would be proof enough of what was supposed to have happened in the room.

He called suddenly, "Virginia!"

A little breathless voice answered, "Yes?"

"I think I'm loosening the screw a little. Will you watch your side and if you see the screw sticking out a bit there will you try and grab at it and pull? It may help to get it out faster."

"Oh yes. Of course I will, Mr. Herbert Baring." She stared hopefully at the lock, waiting for the screw to appear like a little worm coming out of its hole. The thought made her laugh and he asked sharply what she was doing. When she told him the joke he didn't laugh. He said only, "Watch it closely and don't make jokes," so she felt chastened and ashamed.

When the phone suddenly shrilled it was so shocking Aldan jerked away from the lock, speechless for one moment too long. The child had gone. He heard her steps go, swiftly. He called to her, urgently, not daring to raise his voice for fear she'd already lifted the receiver and his voice might possibly be heard in the background.

He waited in sweating agony, not hearing anything else. She didn't seem to be speaking at all. Then there was a muffled bang and her steps came back.

She was laughing again.

He said, fury in his voice now, "What the devil were you doing?"

He knew he'd made a mistake and could guess she was

standing there the other side of the door, shaken, wide-eyed and puzzled. He said more softly, "Where did you go to, Virginia? I'd just managed to thrust it towards you and now it's clicked back. You weren't there to pull."

She gave a little wail. "Oh, I'm sorry. I'm truly sorry! But it was the phone. I ran and ... it was Mr. Robbins." Laughter was back. "He was mad as mad. He kept saying, 'Are you there, Miss Tarks? I've had a serious complaint. Mrs. Gilbert in 24 is complaining about all that paper in the court. I told her it's your doing, for letting that Virginia drop things ...' He went on and on like that, Mr. Herbert Baring. It was so funny. I just put down the phone, bang, without saying a word to him. I don't need his help now, do I? So I never said a word. Never told him about Miss Tarks or anything, 'cause I don't need him now, do I?"

CHAPTER NINETEEN

The old cat, Robbins thought furiously. Who did she think she was? Slamming down the receiver so his eardrum was nearly busted, was the limit. She must've learned her manners in the gutter, he told himself bitterly.

He fetched out the bird, surveyed it grimly and slammed it on the table. She'd had her chance, he told himself as he carved into it. He wasn't going to bother any more. He'd clean up the mess himself, and straight after the holiday, when the agents came round for their usual inspection, he was going to trot it out, along with the newspaper the kid had sent down the chute, and mention of the stuff on the window, and all the waving and yelling. He was going to say plenty. Both Miss Tarks and the kid and her father would cop it, and serve them right.

He wondered suddenly what Miss Tarks was having for dinner. It wouldn't be a bird like his, he could bet. She liked her creature comforts that one. He did wonder though if the kid would share in it. He was suddenly sorry for her. After all, he reflected, it was Christmas Day. For all of that he had the idea Virginia was getting cold cuts and hard biscuits.

He tried to convince himself he didn't care, and was astonished to find conviction wouldn't come.

. . .

Aldan was standing upright now. He had left the lock because there were more important things to do. There was suddenly a great break in the chain of luck that had so far bolstered him up.

The damn brat, he thought furiously, trying to work out what the man would make of that slammed-down phone.

He'd think it was Miss Tarks who'd done it. That was

clear face. But later ... he'd know then it couldn't have been Miss Tarks. He'd know it must have been the child.

And he'd know there was something wrong. He couldn't fail to, Aldan reflected bitterly. A child who'd tried desperately to attract attention, to break a lock, wouldn't hear a voice and slam down the receiver without a cry for help going across the line.

It simply wouldn't add up—except to there being something wrong about the set-up.

There was a soft knock from the other side of the door. The child's voice sounded bewildered when she asked, "Are you still there? I can't hear you working any more."

He went slowly back. He said, "I'm here, Virginia. I was having a break. I'm not small like yourself. I have to kneel to get at the lock and my knees were aching. My back, too."

"Oh, I'm sorry!" She sounded really distressed. "I won't go away again, I promise. And it was only Mr. Robbins. He was horrible before. He wouldn't listen."

"What?" he jerked.

"He wouldn't. I cried and cried to him to come and get me out and he laughed and he said I deserved locking up because I'd broken the crystal bowl..."

As he listened relief came welling back. It was all right, he told himself. Perfectly all right. It was going to fit in. The child had been let down already by Robbins. It was likely enough that tired and exhausted, recognising the voice of an enemy who'd refused help before and who was now upbraiding her again, she might let the receiver simply bang down again.

And ... Robbins was unlikely ever to tell.

That was what he could count on completely.

The man had refused help, had laughed at her throwing things, had laughed at her pleas over the phone. Never in a thousand years would he admit, once she was dead, how he'd refused to help her. He'd know, if he did, he might be rent to pieces by public opinion. Whatever he thought ... and he'd think that as he'd failed her she'd been too tired to try to get him again to help ... oh yes, it fitted. The caretaker would never speak out.

That was the point to hold onto. He might admit thinking she was locked up for being naughty, but he'd never, never admit to that phone call when he'd laughed at her cries and pleas and gloated in malice.

With renewed energy he bent to the lock, calling, "Later on you can say what you like to Robbins, Virginia. For now, you watch in case the screw pops out on your side."

It was only a few minutes later she cried triumphantly, "It's popped, Mr. Herbert Baring! It has, and I have it. If you push a bit more I can pull. I'm sure of it."

"Right, Virginia," he braced himself. "I'm going to push when I count three. You be ready and pull."

He was smiling, and she was laughing, clapping her hands in excitement, as the screw gave, as he put the key into the lock and turned it, and the handle.

. . .

"The trades hatch!"

Megan saw the two men staring at her in astonishment. She saw Leigh start towards the hall and said, "No!" and saw him stop, his expression mocking her. "I don't mean yours, Leigh. I mean the one at Miss Tarks' flat."

The mockery grew in his eyes. She grimaced. "Look, this is what I really meant. Oh you needn't look superior and start laughing—I know I sound noddle-witted, but ... if we ring or go down to Miss Tarks' place after lunch I wouldn't mind betting she'll be snoozing. Old people love a snooze after a big meal ..." she stopped, her cheeks reddening.

Leaderbee grinned, "You're so right. You wait till you see what I do after your cooking when you're settled in at my place. I told you, didn't I, I snored?"

She smiled back, "Well then, she's going to be quite ... ratty ... if we wake her up. She certainly won't be co-operative—in fact she might get angrier than ever. So ... I thought of the trades hatch. Look, how about us going back —with the bottle of sherry and the squirrel for Virginia.

We'll ring the bell and if she doesn't come we'll slip a note under the door. She's sure to check the chain is on before she has a sleep and when she sees the note ... well, we'll tell her in it who we are, and tell her too look in her trades hatch, and that we'd like to come down later and take Virginia off her hands, to go visiting with a magician, and we'll ask if she'll please ring here and say if it's all right or not.

"Where's the harm in that? She can't possibly take exception. She'll have to ring out of common politeness. Even if she says no to Virginia coming, there's tomorrow ..."

Leigh, she saw with contentment, was already turning down the gas, and Mr. Leaderbee was smoothing down his hair and neatening his tie. They collected the bottle and the little tissue-wrapped parcel, scribbled a note and marched out of the flat, arm in arm.

It was only a faint disappointment that the door wouldn't open to their ring. They opened the little hatch in the wall near the door, put the parcels into the small cavity that was bolted on the other side, closed their side, slipped the note into place and turned away.

Megan said then, "Wait a bit. I put the note under with a corner sticking out this side, so I could see if she takes it in at once. If she does it'll be human nature to open the door and look out to see if we're still around."

They stood there, silently. In a minute, the little corner of white vanished under the door. Megan laughed in delight. She went back to the door, almost running, waiting impatiently for it to swing wide and let her in.

She went on waiting, while the two men joined her.

The door didn't open. In a few minutes more a tiny corner of white came slithering under the door as the note was replaced in exactly the same position.

"But it's absurd," Megan whispered. "Utterly absurd." She flung open the hatch. The things were still there, untouched. She turned away, tears pricking at her eyes. "We know she's not out, Leigh. Why does she want us to think she is?"

. . .

It had been so easy, Aldan reflected. Easy, but still quite tiring. Her coming to him, when the door had swung wide between them, was a rush, a hug, a clinging to him that he didn't try to dislodge. When he pulled her into his arms and carried her she didn't try to get away. She babbled, pressing her small body against his, talking of Robbins and her father and how clever her rescuer was, never apparently noticing the still body on the white sheepskin rug.

Even when he tossed her down on one of the beds she only giggled and cried, "Oh how lovely—how lovely and soft!"

His hand hit her neck almost gently and she went limp at once without even knowledge in her eyes or a cry in her throat. He used a small towel from the bathroom to gag her, and the two bath towels to fasten her arms and legs, then he bundled her round in an eiderdown and left her till he dealt with Isobel.

He used the sheepskin rug to move the body. It meant not moving her from her rigid position, or having to hold or touch her. The rubber backing to the mat moved easily over the carpet, and when she was in the kitchen he went back to the other room to brush up the flattened pile so there was no trace of her dragging passage.

He was still at that when the door bell rang. Shock held him rigid for a moment. Only the knowledge that whoever it was couldn't possibly get in because the door was chained, stopped him crying out, panicking.

He went softly to the doorway, looking into the tiny hall. He saw the white folded sheet come crookedly under the front door, and knew, from the rattle and bang, that the trades hatch had been opened from outside.

He stood there, pondering over it, deciding finally it was something Isobel had ordered, that had come, along with the bill. To make sure he went silently down the hall, sliding the white sheet free and unfolding it.

The words were a shock. He felt them an outrage. What prying fools people were, he thought. Prying stupid fools. But it didn't matter. They'd have no answer. When the door was finally opened it would be by the caretaker with his master key. He'd step on the note and later it would be read, and afterwards these prying people would sob and weep and tell everyone how terrible it was that they'd never known the little girl was in trouble.

Carefully he slid the envelope back in the same position in case they came by a little while later and saw the bit that had been outside was now out of sight. He was pleased at that touch of detail.

He went back to the kitchen then and gently, with the greatest of effort, he managed to ease the mat from under Isobel, leaving her on the kitchen tiles. When he had finished she didn't look as though she'd been disturbed at all since she'd died.

There wasn't even the question of there being no blood on the floor to worry about, he realised in relief. There were only two spots on the white sheepskin and neither were big ones. He'd shot her as she'd been half turning from him in astonishment, about to run, so he'd thought. The bullet had caught her in the back. It had made only a neat hole and what blood there had been had soaked into her clothes.

Just the same, he considered, the sheepskin rug would have to be taken from the flat, just in case. He rolled it, tying it with two lengths of string he found in one drawer and put it out in the hall to collect on his way out.

Satisfied with what he had so far done, he went back to the door that had been locked and carefully inspected it. There were a few scratches round the lock, but when he rubbed them with crumpled newspaper, they seemed to disappear. He inserted the key from the lounge room side and found the lock still worked perfectly.

With a sigh he knelt again, and began to work at the screws holding the knob to the shank on the kitchen side.

. . .

"If you ask me," Megan said flatly, "the woman's not normal. What's the point in putting the note back like that —wanting us to think she isn't in? She must realise we know the child's in. It's ... crazy!"

No one answered her. She thought, They're as disturbed as I am. It *is* crazy. Why on earth should anyone do such a thing, carefully replacing a note that way? Why try to make us believe she's out, when it's obvious that she isn't?"

Her thoughts spun round and round on the same track of utter bewilderment.

She said suddenly, "She's not going to let Virginia out. She doesn't want to. Virginia's going to stay locked up all day—all *Christmas* Day. That's the point of this. If later on we say anything, say to her, 'but Miss Tarks, even if you were ill'—because I'm sure she'll claim she was and that she locked the child up because she couldn't cope with her—'we'd offered to take the child off your hands', she'll give back smartly, 'But Miss Tremont, I didn't know about your offer. I was in bed. I never so much as saw your note at all'."

She swung round to the other two, her eyes bright with indignation, "Don't you see, when it's pointed out? That's exactly what she'll do. If Virginia is just tiresome a normal person would be glad to be rid of her, but Miss Tarks ... she's not normal at all. She's having the time of her life feeling her power over Virginia, gloating over depriving her of Christmas Day—knowing ... there *are* people like that, Leigh ... and ... Virginia's being robbed of her Christmas. She'll have to wait a whole year for another. Miss Tarks knows it and she's glad about it.

"She's ... abominable!"

She felt Leigh's hand touch hers, but she didn't want to be comforted. She wanted to go on feeling indignant and disturbed and terribly angry. To let herself be comforted would be to let herself be soothed into forgetfulness. She didn't want to forget. She wanted to do something—something sensible, worthwhile, for Virginia—to give her Christmas back before it was completely gone for another year.

Moving away from his touching hand she went back to the window, sliding the curtains aside, looking out across the court. The child wasn't there any more, but she was convinced she was in the room beyond, behind a locked door still, just the same.

She went on staring, then asked over her shoulder, "What's that on the window?"

Leigh came to stand beside her. "Looks as though the kid's been amusing herself scribbling or something. They're letters I think ... back to front to us of course ..."

She said sharply, "Leigh!"

His hand was over hers now, tightly. He said, "Yes, I see it too. Now. She's written Help, hasn't she?"

"It's horrible. *That* wasn't done in fun or temper, Leigh. That would be desperation and despair. A job like that—I wish I could see better, but I don't think it's scribble with paint or crayons—it looks like the sort of thing you'd do with sticky tape—Christmas tape. A child wouldn't cut tape into strips and go to all the trouble of sticking it on the window for fun. It would be a terribly big job for a ... how old is she?"

He shrugged, admitting, "She can't be very old. Not old enough to find that an easy job, I agree. Yet she did it. Yes ..."

"Oh yes, you can see, too, that it was desperation—the knowledge she was losing all her Christmas. Perhaps ... oh, Leigh, she mightn't have been allowed to open her presents! The more I think about it the worse it is. Perhaps she'd been told she's not going to be let out all day.

"Leigh," she swung round. He was standing so close to her she almost bumped her face on his chin. He didn't move, didn't take his hand from hers as she went on rapidly, "I'm not going to leave it go. I couldn't. It's abominable and that old woman's not fit to have charge of a child. I'm going to offer to take her for the rest of the holiday. If she won't agree I'm going to find out where the father is and get hold of him and make him agree to it."

"Haven't you forgotten Miss Tarks won't open the door? I bet she won't answer the phone either. Only the child will."

She shook her head. "I'm not going to phone. Or try ringing again. We know that won't help. I'm going to get in. Oh yes, Leigh, we can. The caretaker must have a master key to the place. You needn't shake your head. Those keys are in case of trouble—I know about them. I stayed at a place once where one was used. Even if the lock bolt is pressed down they still open it. They have to be able to do that in case of illness or accident inside the rooms."

Leaderbee broke in, "He won't give you the key, I can tell you that. Be as much as his job was worth to say yes to you, Miss Megan, and that's flat. He knows about little Virginia being locked up and he doesn't give a damn about it."

"Doesn't he? I'll make him. I'll tell him we think there's something desperately wrong—that the woman doesn't answer. We won't say that note was taken in and pushed out again. We'll say we think she's hurt or ill and the child is trying to get help.

"We'll take him outside and point out that notice on the window to him. Why Leigh, now I come to think of it, even the way she threw papers . . . that was desperation too! We'll make Robbins believe that. We'll tell him if he won't agree we'll have to get the police."

The old man, she saw vaguely, was looking alarmed. Leigh didn't look anything but blank.

She waited, her courage, her defiance, slowly evaporating, knowing that if the two of them refused to back her up it would be impossible.

CHAPTER TWENTY

Tentatively Aldan tried the door knob, then nodded. His thoughts were not really on what he was doing—they were centred on New Zealand, in the Southern Alps. Down there, in the clear air, he'd soon be starting all over again. Not even the thought of the vanished money worried him now. Let Greta keep the traveller's cheques. She might be grinning at the moment, but she'd cry later on, when she couldn't find him, and couldn't cash the unsigned cheques either.

And if the authorities ever caught up with him it would only be because she wanted her alimony. What more likely than that a bitter ex-husband should walk out and leave her with unsigned useless cheques, out of sheer spite. He thought that the police might even be sympathetic to him if they did catch him for that, and slap a summons on him.

He was reflecting as he straightened up again and put his pocket knife back into his pocket, that he might try hotel work for a while. That way he'd have free board and lodging and would be able to save what he earned. There'd be tips too, to swell his pockets a bit. Later, when he had a reference he'd try something else—store work again perhaps.

The main thing was that now he had all the time in the world, with no worries. He hadn't really worried before. They couldn't have proved he'd killed Isobel. They would have looked a bit silly claiming in any court that after three years and ten months in prison, after six months of decent living parole, he'd still been so jealous of his ex-mistress he'd suddenly killed her. It wouldn't have sounded sense, and they wouldn't have known the real reason for his action.

Greta had panicked him, of course. He'd been frantic at the idea the police would have been able to pick him up immediately for questioning—and naturally they'd want to do that, even if they couldn't prove anything. But even then his story would have held together—his wish, once he was free of parole, to start all over again with new name, new country.

But whenever he thought of what would have happened if Greta hadn't caught up with him, he felt so sick he retched.

He remembered his wild panic at the airport and could laugh at it, realising now all along fate had been looking after him, carefully protecting him from trouble.

Good lord, if he hadn't woken that morning and seen the message and the child . . .

She hadn't recognised him as the man who had looked into the kitchen on Christmas Eve. Or else she'd forgotten about him. Either way she hadn't looked at him as though she'd seen him before.

But she must have heard plenty. They'd been able to talk quite easily through the locked door. If she'd put her ear to it last evening while he'd talked to Isobel, she'd have heard everything and could repeat it.

But it didn't matter.

Nothing mattered now, except getting her, putting her small hands round the gun and dropping it and then dropping her, then going out, giving a tug to the handle and slamming the door. When the police came the shank and one knob would be lying on the living room carpet and the other knob would be on the tiles beside Isobel's body.

Moving softly he went to the window, standing there out of sight, looking down.

He frowned, wondering in irritation how long the man would be. He went on standing there, wishing he could smoke, but not daring to for fear the smell would remain and be noticed later on, as an alien thing in the set-up, watching the caretaker move round the courtyard, slowly wielding the broom.

. . .

The dishes could wait. He'd better, Robbins decided

grimly, get down to clearing up the courtyard before someone else complained or the managing agents looked in. Not that he could be blamed. If they tried to...

He got out the broom and his apron and went striding out into the courtyard, grimacing as he looked at it. It was frightful all right. There were even bits of papers caught now on the branches of the tree, where the wind had lifted them and dropped them. That, he thought glumly, would mean getting the ladder out and fishing them down.

He gazed up, at Miss Tarks' window. The wretched brat wasn't visible. That was one thing to be thankful about. He wouldn't have put it past her to wait till he'd tidied up completely and let fly with another blast of paper to clutter everything up again, while she sniggered away to herself at his rage.

He told himself that if it happened he'd have a Stroke.

He dwelt almost pleasurably on the outcome of that. There'd be a good rest for a start, and then they'd have to pension him off. Any court in the land, he told himself firmly, would award him a whacking good pension—they wouldn't be able to deny his work had brought on the stroke, what with all the annoyances and frustrations, and the rising blood pressure it had led to.

Getting down to work he kept one eye on the window on the sixth floor. At the slightest sign of her, he told himself, he was knocking off. Till she was out of sight again, that was. He was only going to work when it wouldn't be a temptation to her for some more devilment.

But it looked as though she was eating her Christmas dinner with old Miss Tarks. He wondered how much merriment the pair of them were getting out of it, and what the old girl had actually cooked.

His broom became still.

He stared up at the window again, frowning.

Now that was funny, he reflected. It was the kitchen window. Why hadn't he thought of that before? And yes ... there was that newspaper she'd sent down the chute, too.

Yes, he told himself, she must be locked up in the kitchen

all right, and that didn't make sense. How, he wondered in astonishment, had the old girl cooked the dinner?

He shook his head, reflecting that perhaps she hadn't. She might be waiting for the cooking job till the evening. The kid might be having bread and dripping for Christmas dinner to pay her out.

But when you came to think of it, he told himself slowly, it still didn't make sense. That glass for instance. *That* was in the kitchen. He'd seen it there himself that time he'd poked around in there. There was a whole cupboard full of it—beautiful expensive pieces, he remembered.

You couldn't make sense at all of locking up a kid who'd broken one piece in the very room where she could up and break up the rest out of spite.

Then he told himself that of course you could always lock your cupboards.

Then he remembered there weren't any locks on them. They weren't supplied on kitchen cabinets. In all the units there were just knobs and handles, but no locks on the kitchen cabinets.

Faint uneasiness mingled with the puzzlement as he went on reflecting how absurd it was to lock up a child in the one room in the place where she could do most damage. He turned quite pale at the thought of all the mischief she could have done—turned on the gas taps and filled the place with gas for instance, bringing the gas company and the fire brigade in case of explosion, and having everyone turned out of the building till they discovered where the gas was coming from. He shuddered. What a mess that would have been. There was the water too—he could just see her jamming the plug in the sink and then turning on both taps and gleefully watching the water overflow and make a lake.

And then there were the things like saucepans and dishes. He shuddered again, picturing them thudding down all over the court, and on top of his own head.

His mouth gaped slightly as he gazed up again.

It didn't make sense at all, he thought in something approaching outrage, his mind dwelling on the thought of all the impossible things she could have done up there.

Then suddenly he laughed. He remembered how Miss Tarks had come into the flat and found him poking around in her kitchen. She'd had a fit. In spite of his talk about gas leaks and duty and his rights she'd made him stand there turning out his pockets as though he might have them stuffed with her silver. Lord, she'd been ratty, he remembered with grim relish.

He could bet his socks that after that episode she'd called in a workman and had locks put on every cupboard and drawer in the confounded place. It would have been just her cup of tea.

That, of course, still left the question of the water and the gas, but with a few good threats of what would happen if the kid had played with either even the Segal brat might have had qualms at touching them.

Come to think of it—he bent again to the task of sweeping up the rubbish—it wasn't so bad a place to put a kid if you didn't happen to want the kitchen yourself. There'd be no calls for drinks of water even, as an excuse for getting the door open. And in the bedrooms she might have started rooting in cupboards and upsetting bottles and jars and heaven knew what.

He nodded. The kitchen, after all, was the best place for her. Miss Tarks was quite right.

. . .

He might as well deal with the gun, Aldan reflected. The caretaker couldn't take very long in his sweeping. He must resent the job of cleaning up at all, on a holiday. He'd almost certainly skimp the job and hurry off to his television set or his wife or his friends or whatever he had planned for the rest of the day.

Carefully he rubbed over the gun, then still holding it in his handkerchief he went into the bedroom. The child was awake. Her eyes looked enormous.

He said, "There's no need to worry, Virginia. I'm going to roll you over for a minute."

He had tied her arms above the elbows. Her small hands were easily lifted and forced into position about the gun. In fact she held tightly to it, so he had to drag it free. All the better, he thought complacently. Blurred prints would be more effective than clear ones.

He rolled her back, looked into her bewildered eyes and thought he had better make up some story to satisfy her till he could deal with her. There was no need to torture her with speculation and fright. He was even remotely sorry for her.

"There's no need to worry, Virginia. You're comfortable enough, aren't you? In about fifteen minutes—can you count that much?—you'll be free again. You see, Virginia, I'm not exactly what you thought I was. I happen to be ... a burglar."

He saw her eyes round with astonishment, but the faint fear drained out, leaving only that astonishment mingled with bewilderment.

"Christmas Day my sort of person is extra busy as a lot of places are empty," he told her. "We know we'll have a free hand in them. We knock on doors, you see, and where there's no answer, well ... we go inside.

"So I came in here. Then I realised you were shut up. Well I couldn't have that, of course. I had to set you free. But Virginia, I still had my job to do, you know. I've nearly finished. Soon I'll go away and then I'll ring the caretaker of the building, or the police, and tell them there's trouble here, and to come up and rescue you. So you see, there's nothing to worry about. I'm sorry to disappoint you about myself, but ... there it is."

She was shaking her head, violently, from side to side, her great eyes accusing and angry now.

Because he was puzzled, and there was time to waste somehow or other, he took the towel from her mouth.

She said, after licking at her lips with a small pink tongue, "You knew my name. How did you know *that*?"

Knowing a moment's bewilderment, he was silent, then he smiled. "Didn't I tell you I was down in the courtyard, looking at you, and talking to the caretaker and that he told me about you? I was looking up at the windows you see—noticing if any were locked and bolted. We do that, Virginia, because it tells us who might be out and away from home. Understand?"

She looked interested now. Interested and even, he realised in wry amusement, faintly admiring.

"I only rang your bell, or rather Miss ... what's her name's ... bell, because the lady next door said the place was empty. Oh yes, I ran into her as I walked out of the lift. Rather disconcerting. Do you know what that word means? It means I was surprised and startled and put out at her seeing me. But she gave me valuable information. She said she'd been ringing and ringing at the bell here and you must be out because she couldn't smell any dinner cooking either, though she'd put her head out of her window and sniffed towards your kitchen. Rather clever of her, wasn't it?

"It was a little time since I'd seen and heard about you. I thought—now here's a place that's right for me. So I came in. And when I heard you and found the door locked and Miss ... what's her name ... on the floor ..." he saw the question in her eyes, answered as he had done before, "Yes, she's dead. I'm sorry. There's not a thing anyone could do, or I'd have sent for help, wouldn't I?"

"It was Heart," Virginia said wisely. Her brief fear and her long bewilderment were all over. She hardly thought of Miss Tarks. She was thinking only of getting back to school and telling everyone of this impossible Christmas—all about being locked in, and all the things she'd done, and how stupid Robbins had been, and then her meeting with a real-life burglar who had told her how people like himself went to work, and about the tricks of his trade.

She felt like giggling at the idea of burglary being a trade, but then she asked, quite politely, because she was tired of being on the bed and she wanted, so much, to be free and made a proper fuss of and everything to be over, "Will you be very long, Mr. Burglar?"

"No," Aldan moved towards the door again. "No, I won't be long, Virginia—not long at all."

CHAPTER TWENTY ONE

Robbins shook his head. He went on shaking it, closing his eyes, refusing to look at them. If he kept it up, he thought wearily, they might go away.

Really it was too much for anyone to expect him to stand, he reflected bitterly. First it was Miss Tarks, then the kid, then the old fellow ... and what right had he to come back like this and start demanding keys and raging on about there being something wrong upstairs? There'd been Mrs. Gilbert's complaints too, he thought, feeling more tired than ever. Then that wretched roast sparrow that had cost the earth and shrivelled to nothing.

His eyes opened. He said viciously, "I don't care a damn what you think. Any of you. I can't go round the units opening them up because some kid's causing trouble. And I've had enough of Miss Tarks. I went in before. We were having trouble with the gas and I had to go in and look for a leak. That was part of my job. I said so, but oh no—she had me standing there turning out my pockets while she threatened to have me up for breaking and entering. If she hadn't been too much of a prissy old lady she'd have got a bit closer and run her hands over me just to make sure I didn't have a spare fork down my pants!"

He shook his head. "Look, mister, and look..." he turned from one to the other, pleading now, "I can't risk it. She's up there fine and dandy and if I use my key and walk in on her—and her probably lying down in her undies, come to think of it—I'll be out of my job."

Leigh began, "I've told you..."

"Oh yes, you've said you'll take the responsibility, but you can't, Mr. Warner. No matter what you say the responsibility rests on me. The agents told me that when they put me in here. They warned me not to use my key except for what they called a last resort, and that's not this. Oh no, it's not. They told me—Watch it, Robbins. They said folks would come and say they were friends of so and so who was out, and how about letting them wait upstairs—using my key? Or someone in one flat would have a bunch of flowers they wanted to stick next door and the woman there was out ... and so on and on and on," he said wearily. "I was warned. No, I can't use the key. I know and you know the kid's been up to mischief and she's locked up for it. It's not our place to go into the rights and wrongs of it. The fact is ..."

Leigh said quietly, "The fact is I'm stating I think there's something wrong. That should be enough. If someone comes to you and says there's something wrong in another unit, you should investigate. I've pointed that window out to you ... you've told me about that notice she sent down the chute—there's no one could throw you out of your job for ..."

Robbins closed his eyes. They weren't going to go away, he knew quite definitely.

He said almost remotely, "Then I'll do this. I'll ring the managing agents. If they tell me to use my key I'll use it. If they say so, you can talk to them yourself and put your case to them and see if they change their minds." He opened his eyes. He said aggressively now, "What's wrong with that?"

Megan said anxiously, "It's a holiday."

Robbins nodded. "Oh yes, it might take time to get hold of them, but what of it. She's been locked up all morning. Half an hour, or three quarters, or even an hour won't hurt her. Will it now?"

. . .

What the devil was going on, Aldan wondered frantically. He had gone back to the window to peer out and see if the caretaker had gone, and had found him still there, staring up at the window, with two other men and a girl.

It was the threesome who'd written the note, he was certain. Remembering the child babbling of them he thought, Mr. Leaderbee and the nice man with the tree.

But what on earth were they doing? They were going on standing there, while minutes flickered by, and anxiety grew to a frightening knot in his throat.

The caretaker seemed angry, he considered. The man was waving his arms, as though trying to brush the other three away, at any rate. But they were standing their ground, and all of them were again staring upwards, and the younger man was pointing.

For a horrible moment he thought they might have seen him, careful as he'd been not to appear against the glass.

While he watched they went back to talking. Whatever it was all about the conversation seemed never-ending. He wondered suddenly if at last they'd realised what the message on the window really was. He wondered what the caretaker was saying, and if the man was still convinced there was nothing wrong up here, and was convincing them in turn.

He was sure that must be it, so sure that he relaxed, expecting the three to straggle away and leave the caretaker to his sweeping. But as he watched, the four of them, in a huddle, began to move away, the caretaker tossing aside the broom, as though he now had something better, more urgent, to attend to—something that simply wouldn't wait.

Aldan jerked back from the window. They were coming up, he thought frantically. The three had convinced the caretaker instead of the other way round, and now they were going to come up.

Fright made him dither away precious seconds, then he calmed, remembering the door was chained. Even a master key couldn't break the chain he remembered.

Panic swept back, worse than ever, as he realised the chain would have to come off. If they found it chained now, and unchained later on, when he'd left the building, the whole plot would fall to pieces, because a door doesn't unchain itself.

And ... he shook his head savagely, trying to clear the cotton wool feeling in his thoughts that was blanketing out real thinking ... ten to one if they found the chain on some of them would stay there while the rest went for tools to smash it open. Once they had the door unlocked and there was still no reply to their calls and bangs they'd know Miss Tarks couldn't be out because of the chain. Oh yes, he realised, they'd break in.

He didn't dare speculate how much time he had. His wits started working again like clockwork, planning ahead with precision. Open the window first—the widest it would go. He did it, and moved smoothly through the door and across the living room and into the bedroom.

Untie the child, his thoughts commanded. Pick her up and carry her.

He was unprepared for her gasping, "Are you finished?"

He said abstractedly, "In a minute, in a minute. I'm putting you back in the kitchen, Virginia. I'll give you a number to ring. The police it is. You ring it and tell them what's happened and they'll be here in no time at all and they'll unlock the door..."

"Unlock!" The sound was a scream of fright, of despair, "Oh, you can't lock me in, again, you can't, you can't," as she began to struggle, but his grip on her was so tight the cries, the struggles and twistings in his arms changed to a whimpering, desperate appeal, "Don't hurt me. Please don't hurt me so."

CHAPTER TWENTY TWO

Margot Hickens pulled impatiently at her husband's arm, pleading, "Do look, Rog."

His head moved slowly. He said heavily, "Why bother? You, I mean, not me looking. Why bother about her? You've been fretting ever since the damn party broke up."

"Well . . . we were awful. Oh yes, we were, Rog." Her eyes were clouded from their usual clear blue. "I've been wondering all morning if she isn't feeling ill in bed. She might have a migraine or something—well, look at yourself—you can't bear to turn your head, or look at the sun or anything else.

"And after all she's alone in there."

"If her head's killing her do you think you're going to make it better by ringing her door bell off and on the way you're up to?" he asked wearily.

"This will be the last time." She stood back to admire the little basket of fruit she had carefully wrapped in golden cellophane. "It honestly does look pretty, Rog, and it's the sort of thing that would appeal to a person like Miss Tarks. She can't go high-hatting us after this. I bet she was brought up on the principle of always paying your debts. If she accepts this she'll be in our debt, get it?"

"She'll probably come and throw it in your face. Don't blame me if she does. You'll have asked for it."

She shook her head. "I don't think she will. Can't you get it into your head that she can't relish having difficult neighbours any more than we do. Short of us selling our unit we're stuck with one another for years ahead. If there's a chance of improving things and starting afresh with the possibility of a bit of peace and sweetness all round, I'm certain she'll take it.

"So . . ." she drew a deep breath, "Just as soon as I find

some ribbon to go on top I'll take this out and put it in her trades hatch with a note. I'll ring just once. If she doesn't open I'll stick to the hatch. If she does ... well it'll be a big slice of humble pie from me and a lot of gracious forgiveness from her, I bet. You just wait and see if I'm not right."

. . .

Robbins was angry now. It showed in his screwed-up eyes and almost vicious thrust at them, "Why'nt you ring *her*—that brat—again? Oh you needn't look surprised and innocent as though you'd forgotten to do that—you know you're not going to ring her because if you did you'd learn the truth—that she's simply a brat locked up for doing wrong—and then you'd have no excuse for getting into the place, would you?"

Megan said sharply, "All right then. We'll ring her. We'll ring Virginia. I hadn't forgotten we could do that, but ... we gave her a promise before. We broke it. And if there's something really wrong, she could think we mightn't even believe her, no matter how we said we did. We've broken a promise, don't you understand that? She'll be angry with us and ..."

Robbins was pulling at his lower lip. He wished they'd shut up. They were so smart with words he was beginning to think black was white and he was maybe somebody else. He abruptly put out his hand, brushing hers lightly from the phone.

His eyes were still bright with anger as he said slowly, "You know quite well what she'll say don't you? You know real well what sort she is—she'll tell all the lies in the world so long as it got her out. She'll tell us Miss Tarks is lying there with a broken leg, bleeding like a pig and she's locked in and can't help ... oh yes, I'm not so dumb I don't see that now. She'll lie and lie and lie and you and him and him," his finger jerked round the circle of faces, "will 'tend you're believing it and use what she says to make me open up.

"And it'll be *lies*!" His tone was full of outrage now. "Just lies, and you'll know it. Just because she's a kid you're willing to make trouble for everyone to let her out of that room up there. Well, I won't have it."

He was feeling satisfied now. That had shown him, he thought complacently. Him, with his big sticky beak of a nose, and the old fellow too and that girl with her innocent round face and her probing ways. Oh, he'd shown the lot of them and now they didn't know what to say.

He said, defiant now, "I'm damned if I'm going to pester the managing agents, either. A pretty fool I'd look, wouldn't I? Oh no," he shook his head definitely, "you half drowned me with a lot of words, but now I've got my wits back. I'm not ringing anyone or doing anything at all."

. . .

The sound was so shocking, so unexpected, that he was instantly still, clutching the struggling child to him, whispering to her, because it was imperative to quieten her and yet he couldn't risk letting her go, so he could strike her into unconsciousness, "Hush, Virginia. Be quiet. Did I really hurt you?"

Her voice whimpered against his chest, "Oh you did. Please don't lock me up again. I couldn't bear it."

"Hush, Virginia," he whispered, while his mind was concentrated in panic on the front door.

They couldn't have come up so quickly, he was certain. It couldn't be the three sticky-beaks and the caretaker already. There simply hadn't been time for them to get up, so it had to be someone else out there, standing against the door and ringing the bell, someone who'd get no answer and would eventually go away.

But how long would they stay? The question pounded at him, as he thought of the person staying on and on, while he was trapped—completely trapped when the person there was joined by the caretaker and the others, armed with the key.

He said automatically, "Hush, Virginia."

He didn't know now what to do, then he heard the rattle and bang that heralded the trades hatch being opened again. He listened, hearing the door bang shut again.

He drew a long painful breath of relief, realising the person was satisfied, had left whatever they'd brought and now they were hurrying away.

Swiftly, still holding the child, whispering to her, not really knowing what he was saying, only that he must keep his voice soft and gentle and soothing, so she wouldn't struggle, he went to the window.

For a minute anger held him, and then relief.

The sight of the caretaker, back again, had brought rage, because now he couldn't complete the plan, then relief, because it meant that whatever had happened with the other three people, they weren't on their way up, armed with the master key to let themselves in.

I'm safe, he thought, and relaxation brought an absurd ridiculous gaiety, so that he laughed and the child asked, "Why are you laughing? At me? Because I'm afraid of being locked up again? Oh please ... it's all been so horrid, and..."

"Hush, Virginia."

He was going to take time again to soothe her, he reflected. He still had to wait, till the caretaker had gone from the courtyard for good. He couldn't keep hitting the child into unconsciousness every time she came round, so he had to soothe her and keep her quiet.

He held onto her so her back was towards Isobel's body. He asked, "Why are you frightened, Virginia? Didn't you hear me saying I was going to give you a number to ring. You'll speak to a policeman and tell him about things..."

She said, "But what if he doesn't believe me? No one believes me. I've cried and I've called and I've spoken to people... you *can't* lock me up again and go away and leave me locked up and..." her voice broke.

He gave her a little shake, "They'll believe you."

She shook her head dumbly. "Why can't you leave me in the bedroom and go, and when you've gone I'll run out and down and..."

"Oh yes, so you would, and I can't have that. I can't have you rousing the building until I've got well away, Virginia. *I* don't want to be locked up—for years and years and years. That's what happens to people like me, Virginia. If we're caught. And I know what would happen if I left you free—you wouldn't be able to bear wasting a single minute—you'd run straight out ... I couldn't have that.

"This way, you'll have to use the phone and get the policeman and speak to him and talk to him and spend time convincing him your story is true and then it will take more minutes still till the police car comes. If you don't think they'll believe you, I'll leave you here and when I've got well away I'll ring them myself. How's that?"

She said with conviction, "You'll forget. *They* promised and they never came. You won't do anything either. Oh, I won't go back in here and let you ... I won't let you lock me up again!"

Her small hands went to beat at him, frantically.

. . .

Megan said, "Well, we tried. If I drop dead now," her lips twisted mirthlessly, "write on my tombstone that I tried, will you?"

Leigh gave her a little shake, "Why would you drop? Oh don't tell me—I know. You're ready to drop dead from rage?"

"Well, I am. It's so absurd and yet ... he was right, of course. If she's all he says she could spin whatever lies she liked and even if we didn't believe ... but Leigh, I can't believe she's so bad, that ..."

"Even the best of children can tell wonderful whoppers. Megan, are you going to spoil your own Christmas by thinking of nothing else?"

She turned swiftly. Her eyes were bright with unshed tears. "I'm sorry. I've made a fuss and I've spoilt things for you and Mr. Leaderbee too, haven't I? And you're quite right of course—if I go on thinking about it all I'll spoil Christmas for myself and for you ..."

She gave herself a little shake. "I suppose there's nothing else to be done, that's all."

She knew her voice, her eyes, were begging him to disagree—to suggest something else they could do. She knew that his reply was only answering the appeal. She was sure he wanted nothing more than to simply forget about it all. She was even ashamed of herself for nodding eagerly to his simple, "We could have one last try—one last ring at the bell. If you like."

This time it was herself in the middle as they went to the lift, herself with an arm linked each side with other arms, as though now she was the one in need of support, not the old man.

She knew that when they'd had their last ring at the bell the linked arms would smartly turn her and whisk her away down to the fourth floor. She was even glad it was going to happen as they stepped out of the lift.

She saw the woman turn, stop and stare, then say, "Hi, you're one of my neighbours, I think," with her gaze on Leigh Warren, while she patted her hair. "Merry Christmas to you." Her gaze and voice mocked them all, "So you've come back again." When they didn't answer her, one hand began swinging at the long rope of beads at her throat, "And now I've let the pussy cat out of the bag, haven't I?

"I might as well say outright, I saw your note and pulled it out and read it. I saw your parcels too. Oh, I've left them alone and I pushed the note under the door again, too. It *was* you, wasn't it? The note said, 'Three of us—old Mr. Leaderbee, Megan and myself—the man with the baby tree'." She went on swinging the beads. "But who's Virginia? There's no one in there but Miss Tarks and she's Isobel. I know that. I saw it once on a letter. You must have mixed up your flat numbers, hmmm?"

"Ah no," Leaderbee shook his head. "You're wrong, there. There's a little girl. Locked up."

"What?" The blue eyes had rounded in astonishment. Then she laughed, "Miss Tarks with a child! You're dreaming. There's no kid in there."

But her expression changed from mockery and surprise, as Megan's voice thrust at her, telling her of the day, of the evening before when a small hand had fluttered. Megan went on, the words spilling out at the other woman, telling of the child's plea over the phone; her message on the window with its pathetic abortiveness.

The elder woman said at last, "Well, I'll be . . ." she stopped. Her gaze was abstracted. "What an old cat—Rog was right. He said I was being a fool you know." Then suddenly she grinned, a wide pixie grin that made her look much younger, "I'll tell you something—you can still give her that present. Fish it out and I'll show you something."

She led the three of them into the other flat, into the disordered kitchen, throwing over her shoulder, "The place is a pigstye, but I'm too damn tired to clear up. Look at that," her hand flicked down the garbage chute. "That's the garbage chute." When they gazed blankly back she added impatiently, "You said the kid was tossing notes down the chute to old Grumps in the basement, so she must be in the kitchen . . ." her expression changed. "Well that's . . . do you know, I bet the old tartar's gone out and left the poor little devil cooped up in the kitchen—probably with a bun and a glass of water for her dinner—and a lock on the refrigerator to keep the poor kid out of that. But look . . ." she reached behind one of the cupboards and brought out a thin flexible rod, "See that? When we first came into this place I saw that chute and the chute next door weren't far apart—it's the same set-up as at my sister's block of flats.

"Sis and the woman next door are thick as thieves and have a habit of opening their chutes and calling back and forth to one another—the old back garden fence without the back garden!" Her pixie smile flashed out again. "When Rog and I moved in here I thought to myself Mrs. Next-door—not knowing Miss Tarks then—and I could have a similar set-up. It's surprising how easily you can talk when both chutes are wide open. So one fine day poor fool me used the rod to bang on her chute.

"That was the start of our series of rows." She sighed. "She was livid. She told me gossip was common and she wasn't that, whatever I happened to be—oh reams and reams of stuff like that." She dismissed it with a wave of one hand. "I never tried again but we can knock now. We'll call to her as soon as she opens up and tell her to prepare for a surprise. We can tie your present on the rod and wiggle it round to her. We can tie on other things too, fruit and so on—make a regular game of it for her. How's that for a bit of Christmas fun?"

. . .

For one startled minute he didn't know where the noise was coming from—it seemed to fill the whole room with a resounding knock, as though someone was actually knocking on the door between living room and kitchen, though even as he whipped round he realised he was looking in the wrong direction.

But his turn, his loosening hold on the child, was enough to allow her to get free. She screamed at him, "I hate you, I hate you! I won't stay in here!" while she went running round the room, dodging him like a tiny wild animal, her movements too swift and agile for his clumsy, heavy-bodied following.

Triumphantly she dodged under one of his outflung arms, dived for the doorway, was through it, catching at the door as she went, slamming it shut in his face.

Viciously, frantically, he reached out, staggering backwards, hit the cupboard on the far wall and stood there, looking at the knob in his hand, at the steel shank disappearing as he watched, through the door. He dived for it, but his fingers slid over it. He heard the knob and the shank fall on the other side and all he could think of was how ridiculous, how utterly ridiculous it was.

. . .

Virginia went on running, through the lounge room and out into the hall. She managed the bolt and chain easily and went running out, seeing the open door to the flat beyond, running inside, crying out.

She saw startled eyes, saw running people coming to her

while her thoughts were concentrated on the banging she had left behind in the other flat.

She cried to the mouthing faces coming nearer to her, "Look—come with me," and ran back. Her small hands beat on the locked door, "I hate you, I hate you," she cried.

Aldan heard her, and cursed. He wasn't worried about the door. Not really worried. In a minute, when he'd calmed down his rage and his panic he knew he would be able to force back the handle tongue and get out. His thoughts were concentrated on keeping the child there—not letting her run away to get help.

Through the panels his voice cried to her, "Virginia, don't! Hush, Virginia, don't be silly. Didn't you know, Virginia, that it was only a game. That was all. Hush, Virginia. it was only a game!"

OTHER TITLES IN THE SOHO CRIME SERIES

JANWILLEM VAN DE WETERING

Outsider in Amsterdam
Tumbleweed
The Corpse on the Dike
Death of a Hawker
The Japanese Corpse
The Blond Baboon
The Maine Massacre
Just a Corpse at Twilight
The Streetbird
The Hollow-Eyed Angel
The Mind-Murders
The Rattle-Rat
Hard Rain
The Perfidious Parrot
The Amsterdam Cops: Collected Stories

SEICHŌ MATSUMOTO
Inspector Imanishi Investigates

MARTIN LIMÓN
Jade Lady Burning

JIM CIRNI
The Kiss Off
The Come On
The Big Squeeze

CHARLOTTE JAY
Beat Not the Bones

PATRICIA CARLON
The Souvenir
The Whispering Wall
The Running Woman
Crime of Silence
The Price of an Orphan
The Unquiet Night

CARA BLACK
Murder in the Marais
Murder in Belleville

JOHN WESTERMANN
Exit Wounds
High Crimes

CHERYL BENARD
Moghul Buffet

J. ROBERT JANES
Stonekiller
Sandman
Mayhem
Salamander
Mannequin
Carousel

AKIMITSU TAKAGI
Honeymoon to Nowhere
The Informer
The Tattoo Murder Case

STAN JONES
White Sky, Black Ice

TIMOTHY WATTS
Cons
Money Lovers

JANET HANNAH
The Wish to Kill

PETER LOVESEY
The Vault
The Last Detective
The Reaper
Rough Cider